Levi did something he was certain he would regret. He pulled Alexa into his arms.

Despite the situation, he felt the very thing he didn't want to feel.

The heat.

Oh, yes. It was there mixed with all the fresh emotions and spent adrenaline from the latest attack.

"You don't want this," Alexa whispered.

Even though she didn't qualify what she meant by *this*, Levi made a sound of agreement. He didn't want the problems that could come from the attraction he was feeling for her.

But he did want her.

And he did something about it when she leaned back to look at him. He slipped his hand around the back of her neck and he kissed her.

It felt like a truck had hit him in the chest. Oh, man. He hadn't wanted her to taste like something he was certain he could never get enough of. He'd wanted the kiss to satisfy this need stirring inside him.

Didn't happen.

The need soared.

TROUBLE WITH A BADGE

USA TODAY Bestselling Author

DELORES FOSSEN

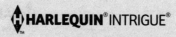
HARLEQUIN® INTRIGUE®

To my amazing daughter-in-law, Dr. Tabitha Fossen

Recycling programs
for this product may
not exist in your area.

ISBN-13: 978-0-373-74950-8

Trouble with a Badge

Copyright © 2016 by Delores Fossen

This edition published by arrangement with Harlequin Books S.A.

For questions and comments about the quality of this book, please contact us at CustomerService@Harlequin.com.

Printed in U.S.A.

www.Harlequin.com

Delores Fossen, a *USA TODAY* bestselling author, has sold over fifty novels with millions of copies of her books in print worldwide. She's received the Booksellers' Best Award and the RT Reviewers' Choice Best Book Award. She was also a finalist for a prestigious RITA® Award. You can contact the author through her webpage at deloresfossen.com.

Books by Delores Fossen

Harlequin Intrigue

Appaloosa Pass Ranch

Lone Wolf Lawman
Taking Aim at the Sheriff
Trouble with a Badge

Sweetwater Ranch

Maverick Sheriff
Cowboy Behind the Badge
Rustling Up Trouble
Kidnapping in Kendall County
The Deputy's Redemption
Reining in Justice
Surrendering to the Sheriff
A Lawman's Justice

HQN Books

The McCord Brothers

Texas on My Mind

Visit the Author Profile page
at Harlequin.com for more titles.

CAST OF CHARACTERS

Deputy Levi Crockett—The last person this cowboy cop wants to help is the woman who nearly tore his family apart. But duty comes first—even when duty is mixed with an attraction Levi doesn't want to feel.

Alexa Dearborn—When her WITSEC identity is blown and hired guns come after her, she has no choice but to turn to Levi, the hot lawman from her past.

Violet McKenna—A newborn who's the target of kidnappers. But why?

Tasha McKenna—Violet's mother, who's been hiding out from her ex.

Elroy Lockwood—The marshal who could be trying to silence Alexa so she can't testify against him.

Scottie Norse—He admits he's obsessed with his ex, Tasha, but he insists he's not behind the attempts to kidnap Violet.

Marcos Culver—A shady businessman about to stand trial, and Alexa is the witness who can put him behind bars.

The Moonlight Strangler—A vicious serial killer who's eluded cops for nearly three decades. Now he has his eyes on Alexa.

Chapter One

Was the killer already here?

Deputy Levi Crockett didn't see anything or anyone suspicious, but he felt the twist in his gut, letting him know something wasn't right. He eased his hand over the Smith & Wesson in his holster and stepped from his truck.

The winter air snapped at him, the bitter cold going right through his buckskin jacket and cowboy hat, but Levi kept walking. Kept making his way to the side of the Outlaw Bar. Not near the door. But to the back so he'd be able to see when or if the killer arrived.

The bar was within a half hour of closing, but eight vehicles were still in the parking lot. No one was inside any of them though. No one he could see anyway. The vehicles likely belonged to the cocktail waitresses and bartender. Customers, too. Maybe one even belonged to the killer.

And not just any ordinary killer, either.

But the Moonlight Strangler, a serial killer.

If the tip from the private investigator was right, the killer had staked out this bar as the site of his next murder and would be arriving any minute now.

Too bad Levi hadn't gotten more notice from the PI or he could have arranged for a better net to catch this dangerous snake. However, the call had come just a few minutes earlier when Levi was on his way home to his family's ranch. He'd literally been driving right by the place, and that was why he hadn't even bothered to call for backup.

Not yet anyway.

He would though if he saw or felt anything to confirm that the PI was right. After all, one of his brothers was the sheriff. Another was a deputy. And they could be there in less than twenty minutes if Levi needed them. Still, this was one killer Levi preferred to take care of himself.

Because it was personal.

This killer had spilled family blood, and he was going to pay and pay hard for what he'd done to all those women he'd murdered.

Levi eased into the shadows away from the pulsing neon bar lights and he listened. Waited. It was hard though to pick through the sounds of the crackling lights, the wind and his own heartbeat drumming in his ears.

But somewhere there was the sound of an engine running.

Because the driver had the headlights off, it took Levi a moment to realize the car wasn't approaching from the street, but rather from the back of the bar. No road there, just a park-like area that the local teenagers used for making out. It could also be the very route a killer would likely take.

Before the car eased to a stop, Levi whipped out his gun and took aim. He froze. And not because of the weather.

A person stepped out of the car, the watery lights just bright enough for him to see her face. Not the Moonlight Strangler, but someone he did recognize. The pale blond hair. The willowy build.

Alexa.

Of all the people Levi thought he might run into tonight, Alexa Dearborn wasn't anywhere on his radar. Heck, she shouldn't be anywhere near him, this bar or the town of Appaloosa Pass.

Because she had a bounty on her head.

Word on the street was that the hired guns who were after her had orders to shoot to kill.

It'd been five months since Levi had last seen her. Marshals had whisked her away into WITSEC to an unnamed place. Given her a change of name, too. But five months wasn't nearly long enough for the memories to fade.

Bad memories.

Of a woman strangled to death. Paige, his brother's wife. And Alexa was right smack dab in the middle of those nightmarish memories and images that began to jolt through him.

Yeah, this was personal all right.

"I'm sorry," Alexa said, her voice trembling.

The rest of her had to be trembling, too, since she wasn't wearing a coat and it was just below freezing. Her jeans and thin blue shirt were hardly fit for a midnight visit on a winter night.

Levi had no idea why she was apologizing, but it did occur to him that she was the reason he was here. "Did you have a PI make a call to me about the Moonlight Strangler?"

She paused, then nodded. "I couldn't think of a faster way to get you here, and I needed to talk to someone I can trust."

"You can't trust me," Levi grumbled.

But he instantly knew it was a lie. The deputy's badge on his belt wasn't just for show. He was the law and would uphold it no matter what the cost.

Even for Alexa.

"I can't stay out here long. I have to get back." She glanced behind her.

Levi wasn't sure where *back* was for her.

"Then you'd better start explaining why you're here because I'm in a hurry, too." He'd just pulled a long shift and wanted to get home.

Actually, anywhere away from Alexa, and a long shift didn't have anything to do with wanting to put some distance between them. He couldn't look at her without thinking of Paige.

"I still had your personal cell number, but I was afraid you wouldn't answer if you didn't recognize the caller. Or that you'd hang up if you knew it was me."

"Is this explanation going somewhere?" he snapped.

"Yes. I tried calling you at San Antonio PD," she said after she cleared her throat. "I didn't tell them who I was, but they said you didn't work there any longer, that just this week you'd taken a job here in Appaloosa Pass."

It was his third day on the job as a deputy. Levi had put a decade of city law enforcement behind him so he could come home and devote more time to catching the Moonlight Strangler.

Well, that was the official story anyway.

Other things had played into it. Things he had no intention of discussing with Alexa, even though, in a roundabout way, she was part of that unofficial story.

"I didn't want to risk calling the sheriff's office. That's when I called the PI, James Moser," Alexa added a moment later.

It didn't surprise Levi that Alexa would remember the PI who'd helped Levi with the footwork on some investigations. After all, James had done a couple of jobs for her, too, when Alexa had still been running her private investigations agency.

"And you talked James into calling me with fake info about a serial killer so I'd meet you here." Levi cursed. Not just because he wasn't going to catch a serial killer tonight, but because he was a thousand percent certain he didn't want to hear anything else Alexa had to say.

"Something went wrong," she said, taking a step closer to him.

Alexa gave another wary glance over her shoulder at the car she'd parked. She'd left the engine running.

"Why are you here?" he pressed, figuring that'd give him the answer to a lot of his questions and clarify her "something went wrong" remark.

The cold air mixed with the slow breath she blew out, creating a wispy fog around her. "I think there might have been some kind of breach at WITSEC. I think my identity could have been compromised."

"This is the first I'm hearing about it." Of

course, he wasn't exactly in the WITSEC loop. "Are you in danger?"

A burst of air left her mouth. Almost a laugh. But there was no humor. "Oh, yes." Another glance over her shoulder. "Look, I don't have a lot of time, but I need your help."

Levi was guessing this was connected to the reason she'd gone into WITSEC in the first place. Because she would soon testify against a very dangerous man.

Marcos Culver.

And Marcos would have his hired thugs kill Alexa if he found her. Heck, he might kill her himself just for the fun of it.

Bottom line—Marcos would do whatever it took to prevent her from testifying at his upcoming trial. Even though the police knew Marcos was connected to another dangerous criminal, a cop killer who'd also been arrested, Alexa was literally the only person who could put Marcos behind bars.

"I'll call my brother," Levi said, reaching for his phone so he could call Jericho, who was the sheriff. "He needs to know what's going on so he can take you into protective custody."

But reaching was as far as he got. Alexa practically lunged at him and caught his wrist. Not the smartest thing she could have done because her hand landed in his zipper area.

Their gazes met.

Held.

Before she drew back her hand as if she'd been scalded. "You can't tell anyone I'm here," Alexa insisted. "I don't know who's in on this."

That wasn't just fear he saw in her eyes. It was terror. And Levi figured they weren't just talking about the possible WITSEC breach now.

"In on *what*?" he demanded.

"Everything," she said on a weary whisper.

All right. That got his attention. Of course, his attention hadn't strayed too far from Alexa since he'd seen her step out of the car. And it wasn't because he didn't trust her.

"If you don't want me to tell anyone, including the sheriff," he snarled, "then what exactly do you think I can do for you?"

"It's not for me," she mumbled, and with her grip still on his arm, she began to lead him toward her car.

Levi got a bad feeling then. One worse than he already had. "You didn't make some kind of deal with the Moonlight Strangler, did you?"

That stopped her in her tracks, and when she whirled back around to face him, it wasn't just terror in her eyes. There was what appeared to be confusion. Some hurt, too.

"I know you don't think much of me." No longer a mumble. Her words were crisp like the air. "But I wouldn't have brought you here to be killed. I already have enough Crockett blood on my hands."

Yeah, she did.

And while Levi didn't believe she'd just hand him over to a killer, that still didn't get him to lower his gun.

"You should know up front that I stole a car," Alexa said. "And that's not even the worst of it. It's possible I killed a man earlier tonight."

That stopped him, as well. "You did what?"

Alexa swallowed hard. "Or at least he might be dead."

Levi motioned for her to keep going with that explanation, but Alexa only tried to get him walking again. When he stayed put, she said something under her breath he didn't catch.

"He was a bad man," she finally continued. "And he murdered someone. He would have done the same to me if I hadn't bashed him on the head with a flashlight." Again, she tried to get Levi moving.

He didn't budge. "What man?"

She huffed, shook her head. "I don't know who he was. A hired gun, I'm sure. And, no, I don't know who hired him. Not yet anyway. But I *will* find out."

That last bit sounded like some kind of threat.

"The guy wasn't alone, either," she continued. "He had a partner."

"You really think he's dead?" he asked.

Alexa pushed her hair from her face. "I'm not sure of much of anything right now other than he came after us. I hit him, stole his car and left him at the gas station at the edge of town. It's closed for the night."

No one had called in a dead body on his watch. Of course, that gas station wasn't exactly in city limits, and that meant Levi needed to get someone out there ASAP to check on the guy.

"If he's not dead, he could have followed you," he pointed out.

"Yes, he could have. And so could his partner. That's why it's not a good idea for us to be in the open. Follow me and I'll explain everything."

Levi just gave her a flat look. She was definitely shaking now. Probably freezing her butt off, but maybe the cold would only get her talking faster, because he wasn't going anywhere with her until she gave him some answers.

"Why come to me?" he snapped.

She stared at him as if the answer was obvious. "Because if there was a breach at WITSEC, then whoever's behind it would figure that you and your family are the last people on earth I'd turn to."

He couldn't argue with that. So, it must have

taken something pretty darn bad for Alexa to make this trek to Appaloosa Pass.

Alexa led him to the back side of the bar. No lights here, but there was enough of a snow moon that he could better see the dark car. Likely the one Alexa claimed to have stolen. And yes, the engine was still running.

"I'm not going anywhere with you," Levi insisted when she tried to get him closer to the vehicle. "In fact, I'm doing something I should have done the moment I laid eyes on you." He took out his phone despite the fact she tried to stop him again.

"You can't call anyone," she insisted.

"We'll see about that. I'm calling Jericho right now. He might not like you, but he'll protect you, and he'll do what it takes to get you safely back into WITSEC."

Alexa got right in his face. "Please. Don't. Just get in the car with me and I'll explain everything. *Please*," she repeated when he hesitated.

Damn.

Levi cursed his hesitation. He also cursed the fact that he was affected in even a small way by her tacked-on *please*. Or maybe it was just the desperation he could see in Alexa's eyes.

But desperate why?

To stay alive?

If so, why hadn't she just taken off in the stolen car and stayed hidden until she was sure it was safe to surface?

Judging from the way Alexa's gaze drifted to the car, the answer was inside.

Levi tightened his grip on his gun and went closer, not sure what he might see. No one was in front, but a heap of blankets was on the backseat.

"She's dead," Alexa said, and a hoarse sob tore from her throat.

The tears came. Man, did they. And Levi cursed himself again when it caused him to reach for her. A gut instinct.

One he resisted.

Barely.

"Who's dead?" he asked. He tipped his head to the blankets. "And is the body on the backseat?"

Alexa sucked in her breath and made another sob. "Tasha's dead. The man at the gas station killed her when he found us. We'd gotten away. We thought we were safe. But we were wrong. *I* was wrong," Alexa corrected. "Her body's at the gas station, too."

Hell. Two dead bodies. "What's Tasha's last name?"

"McKenna. That's her real name. But she's been in hiding for the last couple of months and using a couple of different aliases."

Yeah, he was definitely calling this in.

But the sound stopped him. A whimper of some kind. And then Levi saw the movement of the blankets.

He reacted fast, shoving Alexa aside, trying to get to the injured or dying woman. Alexa had said this Tasha was dead, but someone was definitely alive and moving. Maybe in need of immediate medical attention.

Levi threw open the door, bracing himself to see blood and heaven knew what else. However, it wasn't an injured woman in those covers.

It was a baby.

A newborn from the looks of it.

"You have to protect her," Alexa said, her voice trembling. "You have to tell everyone she's yours. That I left her with you for safekeeping."

And before Levi could even react, Alexa turned and started running away from him.

Chapter Two

Alexa heard Levi curse. He also called out for her to stop.

She didn't.

Couldn't.

If these hired killers were after her, then the best way to save the baby was for her to get as far away as she could. If the men had been after only Tasha, then having Levi lie would keep the baby safe. Either way, it was best if Alexa got out of there fast.

Alexa's eyes were already burning from the bitter cold and the tears she was fighting. Her heart already thudding in her chest. Her legs felt like lead, but she ran as fast as she could.

It wasn't nearly fast enough.

Levi used his football running-back skills from high school to catch up to her within a matter of seconds, and he latched on to her shoulder to whirl her around.

"What the hell do you think you're doing?" he snarled.

"What I have to do to keep that little girl safe."

That clearly wasn't a good enough answer, but Alexa didn't want to take the time to explain. She tried to bolt again. Levi didn't let that happen. He latched on to her, hard, and practically dragged her back to the car. He pushed her against the cold metal of the door and pinned her there with his body.

Which wasn't cold.

Something she shouldn't have noticed.

"Start talking," Levi demanded.

Alexa shook her head. "There isn't time. You need to get the baby to a safe place now."

But he didn't budge. And even in the dim light she could still see the glare he aimed at her. "You had a baby?"

There was plenty of skepticism in his voice. Probably because he didn't consider her the motherly type. It was reasonable. She'd never considered herself that way, either. Not with her stellar gene pool and mess of a life.

"She's Tasha's baby. She gave birth to her three days ago. In secret. She's been hiding from a stalker."

"Tasha," he repeated. "The dead woman at the gas station."

Levi cursed again and let go of her so he could

take out his phone. No doubt to call someone she didn't want him to call. "Don't you dare take off again."

Alexa didn't attempt it, mainly because Levi still had her pinned to the car. He wasn't overly muscled. More on the lanky side. But it was clear he was in good shape, probably because of the backbreaking work on his family's ranch.

"Please don't call anyone and tell them I'm here," she begged. "I think the man who killed Tasha has a police radio. And even if he's dead, his partner could still be monitoring the calls. I don't want anyone to know that the baby's Tasha's. I want everyone to believe she's yours. *Ours*," she added.

"Ours?" he challenged.

She nodded. "I know we were never even close to being lovers, but no one other than us knows that. Whoever killed Tasha might not go after the baby if they believe she's your daughter. Please. Just do this to protect her."

In addition to the renewed scowl Levi gave her, she could also see the debate going on in his stormy brown eyes. He stared at her from beneath the brim of his black Stetson.

"Get in the car," Levi ordered through clenched teeth. "I'll drive the baby and you to the sheriff's office, and I'll call my brother on his personal phone so it won't be on the police radio. Then you can tell me everything, and I mean *everything*."

Not everything.

She couldn't do that. But maybe she could tell him enough to convince him that the newborn on the backseat needed him and his lie. After that, Alexa had to get the heck out of town or else she would put the baby in danger again. It was only a matter of time before Marcos Culver or those thugs found her.

Levi opened the driver's side door and practically stuffed Alexa in, moving her to the passenger's seat. Alexa immediately checked on the baby, who thankfully had gone back to sleep. Maybe she would stay that way until Levi had her in a safe place.

Which likely wouldn't be the sheriff's office, not for long anyway.

Though that was the call Levi made as he pulled out of the parking lot of the Outlaw Bar. Alexa prayed this wouldn't turn out to be a fatal mistake. She kept watch around them, looking for anyone suspicious and wishing that she had a gun. Too bad she hadn't been able to get the one from the man who'd attacked them.

"Jericho," Levi said when his brother answered. "I need you to send one of the night deputies out to the gas station on Shaw Road. There might have been some kind of attack."

Even though Levi didn't put the call on speaker, Alexa had no trouble hearing Jericho's answer. "What kind of attack?"

"Just check it out. My source isn't reliable."

That was a generous way of putting it. And his doubt was deserved. After all, she'd lied to Levi and the Crocketts before.

It hadn't turned out well.

However, she wasn't lying about the attack. It'd happened, all right, and Alexa figured it would take a couple of lifetimes to get the images of the attack out of her head.

"I also need you to find out if there's been a breach at WITSEC," Levi added a moment later.

Jericho paused, no doubt wondering what the heck this was all about. "Give me a minute and I'll see what I can find out. I'll call you right back."

She held her breath, hoping that Levi wouldn't mention her name. He didn't, thank goodness. But he continued the drive to the sheriff's office. Soon Jericho would see her. And he wouldn't be any more pleased about this situation than Levi was.

"You can't tell the marshals I'm here in Appaloosa Pass," she said to Levi when he put away his phone.

"Give me one good reason why."

"Marshal Elroy Lockwood," she provided right away.

Levi knew him, of course. And knew him well. Because Lockwood worked with Levi's other brother, Chase, who was also a marshal. Lockwood had also helped investigate certain aspects of the Moonlight Strangler case. Of course, every law enforcement agency in the state had gotten involved in that investigation in some way or another since the killer had been operating for more than two decades.

"What does Marshal Lockwood have to do with this?" Levi asked.

"Maybe everything. I think he's dirty and trying to hide his involvement in some criminal activity. He could have been responsible for my WITSEC identity being compromised."

And more.

Lockwood could have been responsible for Tasha's murder and those two goons at the gas station.

Levi shook his head, mumbled some profanity. "You have concrete proof that Lockwood's dirty?"

"No, just some talk from CIs, but I can't risk you trusting him. Not until you have Violet in a safe place." Alexa tipped her head to the baby. "If you tell everyone she's Tasha's, at best she'll be turned over to Child Protective Services since

Tasha doesn't have a next of kin. At worst..."
She had to take a deep breath. "At worst, the
killer might come after the baby, too."

Before Levi could give her any assurance that
wouldn't happen, his phone buzzed, and he answered it while he continued to drive. Continued to keep watch, too. Good. Alexa didn't want
that hired thug coming back for another attack.

"It's Jericho," Levi relayed to her right before
he answered the call, but like before he didn't
put the call on speaker. So Alexa moved closer,
hoping to hear what the hard-nosed sheriff had
to say.

"I've got someone on the way to the gas station to check it out," Jericho explained. "And
there's nothing about any problems at WITSEC.
Should I specifically ask about April, though?"

April Landis, a woman in WITSEC who had
an even more personal connection to the Crocketts than Alexa. Because April was pregnant
with Chase Crockett's child. It didn't surprise her
that Jericho would want to make sure April was
okay. Even though Alexa didn't actually know
April, she also wanted to make sure April was
safe. Both April and she had found themselves
in the dangerous situation of having to testify
against men who were linked through criminal
activities. Alexa could get one man convicted.

April, the other. But both April and she had to stay alive first.

"Ask but don't make any waves just yet," Levi answered. "I don't want April alarmed unless I'm certain there's something to be alarmed about. As I said, I'm not sure I can trust my source."

Jericho paused. "This doesn't have anything to do with…anyone else we know, does it?"

Even though Jericho hadn't specifically mentioned her by name, Alexa knew he was referring to her. The venom in his tone said it all. The sheriff hated her as much as Levi did. She could also include his entire family in that hate fest.

And she deserved every bit of it.

"I'll be at the sheriff's office in about ten minutes," Levi told his brother. "I'll explain everything then." Levi hung up and took the road to lead them into town. "And you'll explain everything to me," he added to Alexa when he hit the End Call button.

Where to start?

Better yet, how much to say?

Or not to say.

"This morning I went over to Tasha's to see the baby and her. She'd just gotten out of the hospital, so I thought she could use some help. While I was there, these two armed men showed up and tried to muscle their way in. Tasha and I escaped with the baby, but the men fired shots at us."

Mercy, the sound of those bullets was still echoing in her head.

"Tasha was in WITSEC, too?" he asked.

"No. I met her after my relocation to Austin and we became friends. She'd been in hiding because of a stalker she couldn't shake. A guy named Scottie Norse. According to her, he's a violent, dangerous man, and Tasha was afraid he might try to hurt the baby or use the baby to force Tasha to be with him."

"A stalker," he repeated. "Is that Scottie's baby?"

"No," she repeated. "According to Tasha, she's definitely not Scottie's. And I believe her. She showed me a picture of Scottie so I'd know who he was if I ever saw him around, and Violet doesn't resemble him at all. Tasha said the baby's father was a guy named Brett Mendoza."

"So, how was Tasha involved with Scottie then?" he asked.

"Tasha said she dated him for a while but broke off things when he became abusive. She had him arrested after he assaulted her, but he didn't spend any time in jail. It was his first offense, and he's got money and connections. Tasha moved, started seeing another guy, got pregnant, but then he was killed in a car accident."

He stayed quiet a moment. "So, maybe Lockwood isn't dirty. Maybe the dirt is from this scumbag stalker who sent the gunmen after Tasha."

"Maybe," she mumbled.

Alexa couldn't rule it out, but she couldn't rule herself out, either. After all, there was a reason she was in WITSEC, and she hadn't exactly stayed out of things since she'd been given a new identity.

"Tell me more about these men who attacked you," Levi insisted.

"I didn't recognize them. We escaped in Tasha's SUV, and the men came in pursuit. They chased us for over an hour before they caught up with us at the gas station. That's when they said we should just surrender, that it wouldn't do any good for us to escape because they had contacts and listening devices in the local law enforcement offices."

"And you believed them?" he asked.

She nodded, not trusting her voice for several seconds. "It's not hard to plant bugs or monitor the police radio."

He made a sound that was possibly of agreement. Because he knew it was true. Most small-town police stations didn't do routine sweeps for listening devices.

"If you tell everyone the baby's ours, then

Scottie won't have a reason to come after her," Alexa spelled out.

"If I tell everyone she's ours, then it's going to stir up trouble in my family," he countered.

Definitely. "I'm very sorry about that. But until I know more about the attack, it's the best way to keep Violet safe."

He didn't argue with that. Not verbally anyway. She braced herself for the questions that Levi was no doubt ready to ask.

But Levi didn't ask her anything.

That was when she realized he had his attention nailed to the rearview mirror.

That put her heart right back in her throat, and Alexa whirled around in the seat to see what had put that look of concern on his face.

An SUV was coming up behind them.

"You said you stole this vehicle," Levi reminded her. "But what would the other hired thug be driving?"

"Probably Tasha's SUV. We used it when we escaped from the apartment in Austin. It's dark green." She studied the vehicle behind them, but the headlights were too bright for her to see much.

"Why didn't you use her SUV when you got out of there with the baby?" he asked, snagging her attention.

"The hired gun's car was closer. After they

shot Tasha, I grabbed the baby from her arms, jumped in our attacker's car and got out of there as fast as I could."

Levi sped up a little and then cursed when the vehicle behind them did the same. "Why isn't the baby in an infant car seat?" he asked.

That certainly didn't steady her heartbeat. It started to race again. "Her infant carrier was in Tasha's SUV, and I couldn't get to it before I had to hurry away from the gas station."

Alexa knew where this was going. The baby was vulnerable on the backseat with nothing to restrain her. The newborn was too young to roll over and fall, but a collision could be deadly.

Thankfully, they were already at the edge of town where there were businesses and shops. Yes, it was late and all of them were closed, but maybe the possibility of being spotted would stop the killer from launching a full-scale attack.

Maybe.

"I'll get back there with her," Alexa said, climbing over the seat, and she hoped the precaution was just overkill.

It wasn't.

"We're still a minute or two out from the sheriff's office," Levi said. "It won't do me any good to call for backup now. We'll get there before Jericho could respond. Just hold on to the baby and stay down."

Alexa did indeed hold on to the baby, but she lifted her head just enough to see what the heck was going on. And she didn't like what she saw.

Oh, no. Not this.

The SUV was right behind them, well past the mere tailgating stage. And now that Alexa got a better look at it, she knew for a fact that it was Tasha's vehicle. That meant the person or persons inside had come to try to kill her. The driver didn't waste any more time. He rammed into the car.

The jolt was instant.

It threw Alexa forward, slamming her against the seat in front of her. Thankfully, it didn't do the same to the baby. Alexa put her body over the newborn's, hoping it would be enough to protect the little girl.

There was another jolt.

Then another.

The car jerked to the right, and that was when Alexa realized the killers were trying to force them off the road.

And it was working.

The SUV was much larger, and the driver used that size when he sped up until the vehicles were side by side. Alexa couldn't actually see through the heavily tinted windows, but the SUV bashed right into the driver's side of their car.

"Hold on," Levi warned.

The car lurched to the right as the SUV pushed them off the road and onto the sidewalk. Levi barely missed a concrete bench, but the front of the car bashed into the brick front of an antiques store.

Again, Alexa flew forward, somehow managing to keep the baby sheltered. But the jostling woke the little girl and she immediately started to cry.

Levi started to curse.

Alexa knew why—because they were stopped. They were now sitting ducks. The vehicle was angled so that the front end was against the door of the antiques shop.

"Call Jericho and tell him what's going on," he said, tossing her his phone.

Somehow, Alexa managed to press the Call button, even though her hands were shaking like crazy. Jericho answered on the first ring.

"Levi and I are at Saunder's Antiques Store," she relayed. "And we need help. There's one gunman, maybe more."

Jericho didn't ask who she was or why this was happening. Nor did he ask about the crying baby. "I'm on my way," he said and hung up.

Alexa took the baby from the seat and tried to soothe her. Maybe the newborn wouldn't be able to sense the tension and fear in Alexa's own body. If she did, there was no way she would stop crying.

Levi drew his weapons. Not just the primary one from his waist holster. He also took out a smaller gun from a slide holster in the back of his jeans and handed it to her.

"Use it if you have to," Levi instructed.

Alexa took the gun from him, but she shook her head. "What are you planning to do?" she asked when he opened the car door. "You can't be thinking of going out there. This idiot is a killer, and he might have help with him."

However, Levi was indeed going out there.

He stepped out just as the driver of the SUV lowered his window. Using the other side of the car door for cover, Levi took aim at whoever was in the SUV.

"I'm Deputy Levi Crockett," he shouted over the cries of the baby. "Step out of your vehicle *now*."

She held her breath, hoping the killer would do just that. Then she might be able to learn why Tasha had died.

But that didn't happen.

Alexa caught just a glimpse of the gun in the driver's hand before the shot blasted into the car.

Chapter Three

Levi cursed and dropped down behind the door. But not far. He stayed high enough to deliver two shots into the driver's side windshield of the SUV.

Yes, it was risky because he didn't know if this armed thug had someone else inside with him. Maybe a captive or hostage. But it was even riskier to let the shots continue with Alexa and the baby inside the car.

His shots obviously didn't put the driver out of commission, because the guy fired another shot. Like his other bullet, this one slammed into the door just inches from Levi. That still didn't stop him.

Levi fired again.

And again.

The shooter had to be dodging Levi's bullets because the idiot managed to keep firing, too.

In the distance Levi heard the sirens. Jericho,

no doubt. His brother would be there in a matter of seconds, but Levi was hoping to contain this situation before backup arrived. Each shot meant the possibility of things going from bad to worse.

"Stay down!" Levi shouted to Alexa when from the corner of his eye he saw her raise her head. She looked ready to help him return fire.

Something he didn't want.

He wanted her in as safe a position as she could be considering they were sitting ducks for a shooter. Thank God there only appeared to be one person returning fire, but in this case, one was more than enough.

Levi saw the slashes of the cruiser lights reflected in the shop's windows across the street, and a few seconds later Jericho pulled to a stop behind him. Apparently, the shooter had no trouble seeing it, either, because almost immediately the driver threw the SUV into gear and started to speed away in reverse.

Hell.

Levi didn't want him getting away. He wanted this moron in the interrogation room or else dead so that he couldn't return and launch another attack.

"I'll go after him," Jericho shouted, and he jumped back into the cruiser after glancing into the car. "Get her to the station."

Jericho probably hadn't gotten a good look

at Alexa, but it was likely he'd recognized her voice when she had called him for backup. His big brother wasn't going to like having Alexa back in Appaloosa Pass, especially not with a killer on her trail.

Well, Levi didn't like it much, either.

Just having her here was going to reopen a lot of old wounds about Paige's murder.

Levi fired another shot into the SUV, hoping it would stop the driver one way or another. It didn't. The guy just kept on speeding away.

Even though Levi wanted to go after this killer himself, he knew it was best to get Alexa and the baby to safety. Then he could leave her with one of the night deputies and go help Jericho haul this guy in.

"I'm so sorry," Alexa said the moment Levi got back in the car.

"Don't," he warned her. It wasn't exactly the comforting tone that she needed right now, but it was the best Levi could manage. Adrenaline was firing through him, and his body was still primed and ready for a fight with the gunman.

"How's the baby?" he asked. Since the newborn was crying at the top of her lungs, he hoped that didn't mean she was hurt.

"She's okay. I think the noise scared her, though."

Probably. Those blasts had certainly scared

him. Not fear for himself. But Levi hadn't wanted an innocent little baby hurt because he wasn't able to stop an attack. What he needed to do now was make sure another attack didn't happen, and that started with getting some info from Alexa.

Levi said a quick prayer of thanks when he managed to drive the car off the sidewalk and get it back on the road. The collision with the building front hadn't been a serious one, but it still could have disabled the engine. He didn't want to have to sit there a moment longer, just in case the shooter circled back and returned for round two.

Or rather round three.

According to Alexa, this clown had already killed the baby's mother.

"Did you happen to get a look at the shooter's face?" Levi asked her as he drove toward the station. He didn't speed because the baby wasn't in an infant seat, but he didn't dawdle, either.

"Just a glimpse. It didn't look like the man who attacked us at the gas station or the man I hit with the flashlight."

So, this could be a backup team of gunmen, because it seemed too much of a coincidence for two separate attacks to happen on the same night.

Levi pulled the car to a stop directly in front of the sheriff's office. "Move fast," he warned

Alexa. Just in case someone had managed to follow them. With everything else going on, anything was possible.

Alexa did hurry. She draped the blanket over the baby, and holding the newborn against her body, they rushed inside the building.

The night deputy, Mack Parkman, was at the reception desk, and despite the fact he was talking to someone on the phone, he immediately got to his feet and shut the door behind them.

"You okay?" he asked after he ended his call, but the question seemed to freeze on his lips when his gaze landed on Alexa.

Since Mack had been a deputy at the time of Paige's murder, he knew Alexa. He also knew all the dirty little details about what Alexa had done.

"What the hell happened?" Mack pressed. But then his attention went to the baby. "Do I need to call an ambulance?"

"Not just yet," Levi answered. "But go ahead and call a medic to get down here to check out the baby. We'll also need some temporary supplies—formula, diapers, whatever else a baby needs."

"Don't tell anyone I'm here," Alexa insisted in a whisper. Probably because she believed the threat those gunmen had told her about local law enforcement offices being bugged. "Not the hospital. And definitely no other lawmen."

"Marshal Lockwood called a few minutes ago, right after Jericho left," Mack explained to them. "He wanted to know if we'd seen Alexa because she'd ditched WITSEC."

Alexa sucked in her breath. "Don't tell him I'm here," she said and frantically repeated that to Levi. "And I didn't ditch WITSEC. I think my identity might have been compromised."

"Is that why Dexter Conway's out at the old gas station on Shaw Road?" Mack wanted to know.

Levi nodded. Dexter was another night deputy. "Any word back on that?"

"Nothing, but Dexter probably hasn't had much time to look around yet."

True. That gas station was a good thirty minutes from the sheriff's office and on the opposite side of town from the Outlaw Bar. Still, Dexter should have been able to spot a pair of dead bodies right off.

Mack took out his phone, but it was an uneasy look he gave Levi. A look with questions attached to it when his gaze slid from Alexa to the baby and then back to Levi.

"That's, uh, not your baby is it?" Mack asked.

"Yes," Alexa volunteered quickly. "She's Levi's."

Levi mumbled some profanity and was about to correct that lie, but he made the mistake of looking at Alexa again. She didn't say a word, but her eyes begged him to cooperate.

Damn.

He would. For now. But he'd soon put a stop to all of this, lie included.

Levi just nodded in response to Mack's question.

"Oh," Mack said. "I hadn't realized there'd even been anything between you two."

There hadn't been. And wouldn't be. No way would he get involved with a woman who had a part in nearly destroying his family.

"I need you to wait with her," Levi told Mack so he wouldn't have to explain anything about this relationship Alexa had just manufactured. "I'll head out and see if I can help Jericho."

Mack nodded and made the call to the hospital while Levi got Alexa moving away from the front windows and doors. He took her to his desk in the far corner of the room and had her sit. She didn't stay still, though. She began to rock the baby, and it didn't take but a few seconds before the newborn stopped crying and went back to sleep.

"Just wait here with Mack," Levi instructed. But the words had hardly left his mouth when his phone buzzed and he saw Jericho's name on the screen.

Oh, man. He hoped something hadn't already gone wrong with the chase.

"Are you all right?" Levi asked his brother the moment he answered.

"I'm fine. The driver of the SUV, not so much, though. He's dead."

It was hard not to feel some relief about that. Some. But this meant no answers as to why he'd attacked them.

"What happened?" Levi put the call on speaker so he wouldn't have to repeat the news to Alexa. Maybe there wouldn't be too many gory details. Of course, after everything that'd gone on tonight, she was probably expecting some gore.

"The SUV crashed into a utility pole," Jericho explained. "When I approached the vehicle, the driver was already dead. Gunshot wound to the chest. I'm assuming you put the bullet in him?"

"Probably." Levi doubted someone else was out there ready to kill the guy. "Was he alone in the SUV?"

"Yeah, but there's an infant seat and a diaper bag."

"I'll explain that when you get here." And it wouldn't be a lie. Not this time. Despite Alexa's objections, Levi would tell his brother the truth. He'd have to because unlike Mack, there was no way in hell Jericho would believe Levi had ever slept with Alexa.

"I'll be there as soon as the CSIs and ME arrive to deal with the body," Jericho assured him.

Alexa actually looked a little relieved. Maybe because their attacker was dead. Maybe because Levi wasn't going to have to leave her to offer Jericho backup. It also meant it'd be a while before Jericho got back to the office, and seeing him was likely something Alexa dreaded.

Behind him he heard Mack finish his call to the hospital, but before he could give Levi an update, the phone rang and Mack went over to the reception desk to answer it.

"It hasn't been that long since she had a bottle, but she'll need one in an hour or so," Alexa volunteered, brushing a kiss on the baby's head. "Tasha fed her right before…"

The tears came, and even though Alexa immediately tried to blink them back, she failed. Cursing, Levi rummaged through his desk to find some tissues, and he handed her one.

"Why'd you stop at the gas station where the attack happened?" Levi asked, hoping this would be the start to figuring all this out.

"Because we were running out of gas. I didn't know the place was closed. I also thought I'd managed to ditch the guys following us, but I soon figured out that I hadn't when the car pulled up behind us. The guy had been driving with his lights off, so I guess that's why I didn't see him until it was too late."

Since they had the killer's car parked right outside, Levi would make sure every inch of it was processed. Once they had the identities of the gunmen, then he could work on figuring out why this dirtbag had come after them and put an innocent baby in danger.

Levi eased down in a chair and motioned for her to continue explaining what happened.

"When we were at the gas station, one of the men got out of the car. He was the one who demanded we go with him, that it wouldn't do us any good to go to the local cops. He was armed and came straight for us. We didn't have a weapon, so I told Tasha to take the baby and run."

"And you thought you'd fight this guy off with your bare hands?" Levi knew he sounded skeptical.

She met his gaze. "I figured I'd give Tasha and the baby a chance to get out of there." But Alexa quickly turned her focus back to the little girl. "Obviously, I was wrong. The guy shot Tasha in the back of the head. She didn't fall but more or less crumpled to the ground with the baby still in her arms."

It was hard to hear and it was obviously hard

for her to say it. "And that's when you bashed the guy with a flashlight?" he pressed when she didn't continue.

Alexa nodded. "I hit him as hard as I could and thought I heard his skull crack. He went out like a light. But then the other guy came out of the car, and I knew I had to get out of there. I grabbed the baby, started running and then sneaked back and got in their car when the guy was trying to pick up his partner from the ground."

She was lucky that the second gunman hadn't just shot her in the head, too. Then, heaven knew what would have happened to the baby.

"Why were you coming to Appaloosa Pass?" he asked.

"Like I said, I thought they'd believe it was the last place I'd go. Obviously I was wrong since Lockwood's already called here looking for me."

Yeah, Lockwood. Levi would soon have to figure out how to deal with him. There was no way he could exclude the marshals from this unless he got some solid proof that the lawman was dirty.

"The medic's on the way," Mack relayed when he got off the phone. "He'll bring baby supplies with him. The other call I got was from Dexter. He's out at the gas station now, but he doesn't see anything out of the ordinary. Definitely no bodies or anything like that."

Alexa frantically shook her head and stood, clutching the baby to her. "Tasha was murdered there."

Mack made a sound of disagreement. "Then somebody must have cleaned up the scene real fast because according to Dexter, there's no blood and no signs of any kind of struggle."

"Tasha was murdered there," Alexa repeated, turning to Levi.

"You're sure?"

"Of course I'm sure. I watched her collapse. She was dead."

Maybe. Of course, if the woman had only been wounded and wandered away from the scene, then Levi doubted she'd taken the time to clean up her own blood. Plus, where was the man whose head Alexa claimed she'd bashed in with the flashlight?

"I'm not lying," Alexa insisted. "Everything happened just like I said it did."

Levi doubted even Alexa would lie about a dead body. Still, he wanted proof.

"Should I get a CSI team out to the gas station?" Mack asked. "We've already got one with the DB Jericho found, so we're stretched pretty thin." Clearly, he had doubts about Alexa's account.

Levi nodded, and he hoped like the devil they found something. *Anything.* A CSI search like that would put a dent in the budget. While he really didn't have a choice about ordering such a search, if it didn't produce results, it was going to make him look like a fool for trusting a woman he shouldn't be trusting anyway.

Levi saw the headlights outside the building and figured it was the medic arriving to examine Alexa and the baby. He barely spared the guy a glance. Unlike Alexa. Her attention snapped right to the window.

And gasping, she stood again.

Levi soon realized why.

Marshal Elroy Lockwood walked in.

Lockwood was the sort of man who tended to grab everyone's attention just by being there. For one thing, he was big. At least six foot four. And he had the weight to fill out that tall body. He was imposing, and the stare he gave Alexa was equally imposing.

Except it quickly turned into a glare.

"Alexa," he said, and that wasn't a friendly tone. "Hand that baby to the deputy. *Now.* Because you're coming with me."

Chapter Four

Alexa had to fight through the panic and force herself not to run. She couldn't. Because running would mean putting the baby right back in the line of fire.

Ditto for her.

But she was in hot water either way. If she voluntarily went with Marshal Lockwood and he was indeed dirty, she could be dead by morning. If she stayed here with Levi, the same might happen at the hands of those attackers. And worse, she'd be putting Levi, his family and the baby in danger.

"Why would I go with you?" Alexa managed to ask Lockwood. It was hard to speak, though, with her breath suddenly so thin.

"Because you're still a witness in an upcoming trial, that's why. Or did you forget that?"

Alexa didn't miss the marshal's sarcasm. "Forget that a thug like Marcos Culver wants to kill me so I can't testify against him? No, I didn't forget."

"Good. Because your testimony against him is the only thing that prevented you from being charged with hacking into FBI databases."

Alexa didn't need to be reminded of this. It was true. She had hacked into the databases looking for the Moonlight Strangler. Had gotten caught, too. And to stop charges from being filed against her, she'd agreed to testify against Marcos, who had worked part time for her as an investigator at her PI agency. She'd learned just enough about Marcos to help put him behind bars for extortion and money laundering, though everyone was certain he was guilty of a lot more than that.

But Lockwood might be guilty of those same things.

Both men were free, too. Lockwood because he hadn't been officially accused of anything, and Marcos because he was out on bail awaiting the trial.

"I know you've continued your investigation into the Moonlight Strangler. Did you hack into WITSEC files, too?" Lockwood asked. "Is that how your identity was blown?"

Levi looked at her, silently asking if that was true. Part of it was. She had indeed been running her own investigation, but she hadn't done the rest. "I haven't hacked into anything since I've been in WITSEC."

"But you've been investigating the Moonlight Strangler again," Lockwood corrected.

"Of course I have. He killed a friend of mine and lots of other women. He nearly killed me. I want to catch him."

Something that Levi and she actually had in common. Not that he or his family would consider that common ground. Still, she was hoping that Levi would want to protect an innocent baby.

Even if that protection didn't extend to her.

Alexa didn't bother to hide her frustration. "How could hacking into WITSEC files possibly help me find the Moonlight Strangler anyway?"

"You know there are several people out there who got glimpses of him." Lockwood didn't hesitate to say. "People who asked to be protected and given new identities. I believe you wanted to find those people and question them."

Alexa groaned. "That'd be like looking for a needle in a haystack."

"But it was your chance to find him. Your chance to redeem yourself." Lockwood made air quotes around the word *redeem*.

"How did you even know Alexa was here?" Levi asked the marshal.

Good question, one that Alexa wished she'd

already thought to ask. Somehow she had to force her mind to settle down so she could try to think of a way out of this potentially dangerous situation.

Now Lockwood took his time answering. "When I heard Alexa had skipped out of WIT-SEC I made some calls, and the locals there checked cameras at the traffic lights and saw Alexa driving a green SUV. No one else was in the vehicle, and she took the interstate heading in this direction."

The cameras hadn't shown Tasha because Alexa had told her to get on the floor with the baby in the car seat.

Levi made a sound of surprise. "There are plenty of places the interstate goes other than Appaloosa Pass. Why'd you pick here?"

Lockwood frowned. No doubt not very happy about what was beginning to sound like an interrogation. "I figured Alexa would want to get to a lawman she could convince to be on her side, and there aren't many of those left who are speaking to her. You included. But I figured she'd try to come to one of the other deputies here."

Alexa did indeed know some of the deputies, but it was a stretch for Lockwood to guess she'd go to Appaloosa Pass. Still, he could have figured that it was just what she would do. Of course, the hired guns who'd chased Tasha and her could have reported back to their boss— Lockwood.

"Besides," Lockwood went on. "Alexa would have another reason for coming here. To find an ally to continue her investigation into the Moonlight Strangler."

Again, it wasn't something she could deny. Well, not fully deny anyway. The Crocketts would indeed do anything to catch the killer, but she doubted they'd want any help from her.

"You should have left the Moonlight Strangler investigation to lawmen who know what they're doing," Lockwood said to her like a warning. "You don't even have your PI creds anymore. And besides, even if by some miracle you were to find him, it wouldn't undo the death you were partially responsible for."

At least Lockwood had used the word *partially*, but there were times, like now, when Alexa felt as if she'd been the one to end Paige's life. Paige had been her best friend, and the only reason Paige had crossed paths with the killer was because she'd been trying to help Alexa with the investigation.

Something Alexa would never forget, never forgive herself for doing.

And neither would Levi and his family.

The door opened behind Lockwood, sending

the marshal, Levi and the deputy all reaching for their guns, but it was just the medic.

The man froze. "Uh, is this a bad time?" he asked, eyeing all three of them and looking ready to bolt. He had a bag of what appeared to be supplies in each hand.

"No," Levi said.

At the same time, Lockwood answered, "Alexa won't need your services. I'll have her checked out when I take her in."

Alexa was about to continue her argument that she wasn't going with the marshal, but Levi spoke before she could say anything.

"You can wait in the sheriff's office," Levi ordered the medic, and he turned to Alexa once the guy had scurried in that direction. "What exactly have you been doing to find the Moonlight Strangler?"

It took her a moment to gather her thoughts and switch gears. "Everything I could. Contacting criminal informants I used to work with, following up on any lead I could find. But what I didn't do was compromise my WITSEC identity or any other identities for that matter. Someone else, an insider maybe, is responsible for that." She aimed a glare right at Lockwood.

If the marshal was concerned about that glare, he didn't show it. He seemed to smirk. "Alexa is mistaken when it comes to me. She thinks I once worked the same money laundering operation as Marcos Culver."

"Did you?" Levi came out and asked.

Oh, Lockwood didn't like that. His eyes narrowed. "Of course not." If looks could have killed, Lockwood would have already put her six feet under. "There's not an ounce of proof to connect me to Marcos and those assorted felonies he committed."

Not proof, exactly, but she'd heard it from a CI that Lockwood had indeed been part of the same illegal operation. A part that Marcos might not even know about since Lockwood could have been using an alias to launder money from the sale of illegal weapons. Now, Lockwood might be concerned that his own criminal activities could be brought to light during Marcos's trial. And Alexa would be the one to do that if she could link the information she had about Marcos to Lockwood.

If it was true, it would give Lockwood a motive to kill her, but that was still a big *if.*

"What kind of proof do you have that Alexa is responsible for her identity being compromised?" Levi asked.

She didn't miss the flicker of surprise that went through Lockwood's eyes. "Do you care what kind?"

Levi tapped his badge. "Yeah."

More surprise, followed by some irritation. The marshal obviously wasn't used to having this authority challenged. "The proof isn't something I can share with a small-town cop. Too sensitive. Lives are at stake."

"Yes, including mine," Alexa verified. "Someone killed a woman tonight. A friend of mine, Tasha McKenna."

Lockwood stared at her before looking at Levi. "Is that true? Is a woman really dead?"

"Maybe," Levi answered before she could say anything. "There was an attack and we're looking for her now."

"Dead," Lockwood repeated under his breath. This wasn't only surprise, but rather what appeared to be shock. "Who killed her?"

"I don't have names," Alexa snapped. But Lockwood might know exactly who those men were. "Whoever they are, they also tried to kill Levi and me. What do you know about that?"

Lockwood scowled. "You accusing me of something?"

"Are you guilty of something?" she fired back.

The scowl stayed in place for several more seconds before he chuckled. "Now that's rich coming from the woman who'd do pretty much anything to make things work for her. That includes making up a story about somebody trying to kill you and your friend if you thought it would get you out of being arrested."

Levi stepped closer to the marshal. "Someone tried to kill Alexa. I witnessed it, got caught in the crossfire. Since that crossfire happened in this jurisdiction, I *will* investigate it. That means keeping Alexa in protective custody until I figure out what's going on."

That started a staring match between the two lawmen. One that Mack joined in on when he took up position by Levi's side.

Lockwood finally looked away. "Was a woman really killed?" he asked. "Or is this more of your fairy tale?"

"Someone's out looking for her body now," Levi volunteered.

Lockwood cursed. "You shouldn't have brought anyone else in on this, Deputy."

Maybe Lockwood was genuinely concerned about the possible security breach in WITSEC files. Or maybe he didn't want anyone to know that he was a dirty marshal and trying to cover his tracks by committing a murder or two.

"You don't seem overly concerned that Alexa and the baby could have been hurt or worse," Levi tossed out there.

"Oh, I'm concerned, all right. Concerned that you're believing whatever lies Alexa has been telling you. This is an issue for the marshals," Lockwood argued.

Levi shrugged. "Again, it's our jurisdiction. If and when we have a body, we'll let you know and share what we learn with you and the Texas Rangers."

"The Rangers? Why the heck would you bring them in on this?"

"We sometimes ask them to assist when we're looking at multiple suspects." Levi's attention stayed nailed to Lockwood. "In the meantime, unless you show me conclusive proof that Alexa had something to do with all of this, she's staying here."

No profanity from Lockwood this time. He stared at Levi, then chuckled. Not in a funny, ha-ha kind of way, either. It was laced with sarcasm. "Hell must have just frozen over if you actually care what happens to Alexa."

Care? That was probably too much of a stretch for Levi, considering how he felt about her.

"Excuse us a minute," Levi said, taking her by the arm and leading her into the hall.

"You're not going anywhere with her," Lockwood ordered, but he was talking to himself because Levi had gone somewhere. He ducked inside an interrogation room with her.

"Do you have any real proof that Lockwood's

dirty?" Levi demanded. And yes, he sounded exactly like a cop with that question.

"I heard it from a criminal informant." She didn't have to wait long for Levi to groan, and she knew why. CIs often were not reliable. "Do you believe in gut feelings? Because it's my gut feeling that Lockwood could somehow be connected to Marcos Culver."

Levi pulled in a long, frustrated breath and leaned against the doorjamb. Alexa could no longer see Lockwood, but Levi glanced in the marshal's direction, probably trying to decide whose story he believed.

"You're wasting my time, Deputy," Lockwood called out. "Just hand over Alexa and you can take the kid."

She hoped that Levi heard the menacing tone in Lockwood's demand. Alexa also hoped his tone wasn't her imagination brought on by fear and a major adrenaline crash. But she didn't think it was the latter.

"If Lockwood once worked the same operation as Marcos, then why has it taken him five months to hire someone to kill you?" Levi asked.

Alexa had given this plenty of thought. "I'm not sure. Maybe he recently figured out I could connect him to Marcos. Maybe it took Lockwood this long to find me. I've been living in Austin, but I haven't been staying at the house the marshals rented for me. I've been checking in daily by phone with the marshals as I'm required to do, but I've been moving around a lot."

Levi stayed quiet a moment. "And Lockwood didn't mind not having face-to-face contact with you?"

"Oh, he minded. He was always pressing to see me. Always threatening to undo the deal I made with the FBI if I didn't meet with him. I finally got fed up and called another marshal and met with him instead. Lockwood wasn't happy, and later that day someone trashed the house where I was supposed to be living."

Of course, all of that was still circumstantial. All of it including her own gut feeling. Especially since there'd been a rash of vandalism in the neighborhood where the rental house was located.

"Deputy, I'm waiting!" Lockwood shouted. "Unless you want to be arrested, too, for interfering with a federal officer, I suggest you quit yapping and hand Alexa over to me."

"Please," she said. Something she'd been saying a lot to Levi in the past hour. "Just help me."

But Levi didn't get a chance to answer because of the footsteps. Lockwood came storming toward the hall. Levi met him halfway, walking back into the squad room. Alexa went, too, but she checked over her shoulder to see if there was some way to escape if Lockwood tried to take her. There was.

A back exit off what appeared to be a break room at the end of the hall.

"Now, come on, Alexa." Lockwood's tone softened a little, but there was nothing soft about that look in his eyes. "Just give that baby to the deputy and come with me. Whose kid is that anyway?"

Silence. The kind where Alexa could hear everyone's breathing, including her own.

"Whose kid?" But Lockwood didn't wait for an answer to his repeated question. "Hell, Alexa, did you steal that baby? Because if you did, I'll be taking custody of it, too."

No way would she let that happen, and she silently pleaded with Levi to do whatever it took to stop this. Even if it meant trusting a woman he didn't want to trust.

Alexa waited. Her heartbeat drumming. Every nerve in her body raw and tense. She had no idea how this was going to play out.

Until Levi glanced at Violet.

And then he moved slightly in front of Alexa. "I'm protecting both Alexa and the baby."

Lockwood followed Levi's gaze, and she could almost see the wheels turning in his head. The surprise, followed quickly by the dismissal.

"Whose kid is that?" Lockwood pressed. "Because if he or she belongs to someone in WIT-SEC—"

"The baby's ours. Mine and Alexa's." Levi didn't even hesitate.

More chuckling from Lockwood. "Really? You actually slept with the woman who helped put your sister-in-law in the grave? And from what I've heard, you had a thing for Paige, too."

A muscle flickered in Levi's jaw. "In high school. Obviously, Paige chose my brother. And what exactly does that have to do with any of this?"

"Paige's rejection must have stung," Lockwood said, dodging the question. The smugness was now in Lockwood's tone, and he was clearly trying to goad Levi into some kind of confrontation. "For a while anyway. But I guess Paige figured out she'd married the wrong brother since she was divorcing him."

Levi shook his head. "What I felt or didn't feel for Paige is none of your business."

"No, but what is my business is that I'm not sure I can trust you. Not after what went on at San Antonio PD," Lockwood added. The smug tone had gone up a serious notch.

No quick answer from Levi that time, and because her arm was against his, she felt him tense. Alexa wanted to know what'd happened, but there was no way she would ask in front of Lockwood.

Lockwood, however, didn't let it drop. "What? You didn't tell the mother of your own child what you did?" He'd obviously noticed the surprised look on her face.

And there was no doubt it was surprise on her part. Levi was a top-notch cop, and she figured there'd be only one reason he was here with that deputy's badge—because it was what he wanted.

"We haven't exactly had time to catch up, what with someone trying to kill Alexa," Levi answered. "Can't say the same for you, though. You seem to know a lot about me."

Lockwood didn't break his stare with Levi. "It's my business to know things. When I heard Alexa might be here, I made some calls on the drive over to find out who I'd be dealing with."

"Then it's obvious I'll need to do the same with you." Levi checked the time. "Now, I'll have to ask you to leave. Both Alexa and the baby need to be examined for possible injuries, and then I'll need to get Alexa's statement about the attack."

However, Lockwood didn't budge. "You honestly think I'll just walk out? Or that I believe you're the father of that kid? When exactly did you have the time to get Alexa pregnant?"

"I'd rather not share personal details of my

sex life," she snapped. "Suffice it to say that I was pregnant before I was placed in WITSEC." Thankfully, the lie didn't stick in her throat.

Lockwood continued to stay put while volleying his glares between Levi and her before the glare finally settled on Levi. "You want proof she was involved with the security breach that compromised her own identity, then here it is in a nutshell. Alexa has been contacting anyone and everyone associated with the Moonlight Strangler. Yeah, she used fake names, but it didn't take long for it to get around that somebody, a woman, was searching hard to find the killer."

"So?" Levi challenged.

"So, she reached out to the wrong person." Lockwood looked at her, motioned for her to finish. "Obviously she reached out to someone who learned where she is so that Marcos could get to her."

Levi looked at her, probably to see if that was possible. Her expression let him know that it was. She had reached out to a lot of people, and despite all the precautions she'd taken, it was possible that one of them had connected all the dots and figured out who she really was.

"Here Alexa is, involved in another investigation that might have gotten another woman killed," Lockwood added. "Tasha McKenna, this time."

Levi obviously had a lot to absorb. He also likely had plenty more questions for her, but his attention stayed on Lockwood. "Do you have a warrant or a judge's order to take Alexa into custody?"

Lockwood flinched a little. "Not with me. Didn't think I'd need one."

"Well, you thought wrong," Levi insisted. "Mack, show the marshal out and lock up after him."

Levi put his hand on her back and got her moving toward the sheriff's office where the medic was waiting. He put her inside but didn't go in himself. Instead, he stared at Lockwood, waiting for him to leave. Alexa wasn't sure that was going to happen, but she finally heard the front door open and then shut.

"He'll be back," Levi said under his breath.

Levi was right. Even if Lockwood wasn't dirty, he obviously thought he had a job to do by taking her back into custody. And if he was dirty, then he wouldn't just give up. He was probably heading somewhere now to get that warrant for her arrest.

"You want me to examine them?" the medic asked, drawing both Levi's and her attention to the young man.

"I'm all right," she insisted. "But you should make sure the baby is okay."

She eased Violet onto the desk. Not the most comfortable place for an examination, but it would have to do. It was too dangerous to try to go to the hospital right now, unless the medic did indeed find something wrong. Then they wouldn't have a choice.

Levi continued to volley glances between her and the front door. "I know you only got a quick look at the man who attacked us, but could it have been Lockwood who came after us tonight?"

She took a deep breath, nodded. "He was the same size and weight, and it was just a glimpse so I can't rule him out. But I also can't rule out the most obvious suspect, Marcos."

"Or Scottie." Levi added some profanity under his breath.

Yes, and if it was Scottie, then he'd sent those goons after Tasha and the baby. Levi and she had just gotten caught in the middle. But if this was Marcos's doing, then it was all on her.

Again.

Alexa couldn't stop the nightmarish images from coming. Of another attack. The one that'd left Paige dead.

"God, what if I'm responsible for Tasha's death,

too?" Alexa pressed her hand to her mouth, tried to blink back the tears.

"Don't go there, yet," Levi snarled. Despite the snarl and the tacked on *yet*, there was still something in his voice that she hadn't expected to hear. Sympathy. "I'll get both you and the baby someplace safe so I can start trying to unravel this."

He opened his mouth to say something else, but the sound snagged both their attention.

Violet whimpered.

But it didn't stay a whimper. The baby started to cry.

"She's not hurt," the medic announced, easing the blanket back around her. "There's not a scratch or bruise on her."

"She could be hungry," Alexa suggested. "Or just tired." Heaven knew Alexa was. The exhaustion seemed bone deep now.

Levi nodded, stared at her. "How much do you know about taking care of a baby?"

"Nothing," she admitted.

Another nod, more softly spoken profanity and he glanced up at the ceiling as if asking for divine assistance. They sure needed it and anything else that would keep Violet safe.

"Take the baby," Levi finally said to her. He thanked the medic and picked up the bag of supplies the medic had brought with him. "Mack, we're leaving," he called out to the deputy.

"Where are we going?" Alexa asked, alarmed that Levi was suddenly moving so fast and with a great sense of urgency.

"Someplace you're not going to like." Levi didn't stop. Maneuvering her along with him, he headed for the exit.

Chapter Five

The coffee sucked, probably because it was six months past its expiration date, but Levi drank it anyway. He would have downed pretty much anything right now if it rid him of the dull ache throbbing in his head. Of course, that was asking a lot of mere coffee since the ache was there from worry and lack of sleep.

Especially worry.

For hours he'd wavered between wondering how the hell he'd gotten himself into this mess, and then he'd look at baby Violet and knew the answer was right there bundled up in a pink blanket. As much as he didn't want to be involved in anything to do with Alexa, there was no way he could walk away from the baby.

Well, not until he was sure Violet was safe, and he was a long way from making sure that happened.

He took another sip of the coffee, grimaced

again and walked to the front window to look around. Something else he'd been doing throughout the night.

Levi had alerted the ranch hands that he was in the guesthouse and that there might be trouble, so despite the chilly temps outside, Levi saw several of the men patrolling the grounds. Exactly what he wanted them to be doing. He didn't want anyone sneaking on to the ranch and especially trying to get in the main house.

That was the reason he'd brought Alexa and Violet to the guesthouse and not to the main house or even his own place. He'd recently had a log cabin built, but unlike the guesthouse, it didn't yet have a security system. Plus, it was on the far back edge of the property. Hard to guard.

At least the ranch hands could help keep watch at the guesthouse, because Levi hadn't wanted to bring any possible danger right to his family's doorstep. His pregnant sister, Addie, and her husband lived there full time. Ditto for his mom. No sense involving them in this. His involvement was plenty enough.

His phone buzzed, something that it'd been doing a lot throughout the night, and Levi answered it right away when he saw Jericho's name on the screen.

"Don't ask me again if I've lost my mind," Levi greeted. He'd heard it enough over the past eight hours since he'd called Jericho and told him that he was taking Alexa and the baby to the guesthouse on the ranch grounds.

But Levi thought that maybe he had indeed lost his mind. He just didn't want to hear his brother spell it out again.

"I won't ask," Jericho said. "But the jury's still out on it. How's the baby this morning?"

Levi automatically glanced into the makeshift bed they'd made for her in a large laundry basket that was sitting on the kitchen table. "She's asleep for now. It's a lie, you know. When people say they sleep like a baby, that's a lie. Babies don't sleep much at all."

Levi nearly winced. He didn't often walk on eggshells when it came to his brothers, but Jericho had recently found out he'd fathered a child who was now a toddler. Jericho hadn't dealt with the *pleasure* of sleepless nights because of a newborn and gladly would have traded those hours of sleep for the experiences he'd missed.

"How about Alexa? Did she sleep?" Jericho asked.

"Not much. When she wasn't trying to soothe the baby, she was doing her own share of crying. She's in the shower now." And Levi hoped that would soothe her still tangled nerves.

"Considering the guesthouse isn't much big-ger than an average-sized bedroom, that sounds, well, *cozy*."

"It's not. It's damn uncomfortable." And it was time for a change in subject. "Anything on Tasha or the hired guns who attacked us?"

"No sightings, but the CSIs did find traces of blood at the gas station."

Levi jumped right on that. "Enough blood to indicate a murder?"

"Nowhere near it. But that doesn't mean there wasn't enough before someone cleaned it up. It appears somebody used the hose to wash away the blood."

So, Tasha and the other man could indeed be dead. But why would the person responsible want to move her body and do a cleanup when there'd been a witness to the murder?

Levi didn't have an answer for that, either.

"What about the car Alexa was driving, the one that belonged to the gunmen?" Levi added. "Has it been processed yet?"

"Still working on that, too. There were smeared prints in various places, but so far they're only a match to Alexa."

Not surprising since she'd driven the vehicle, and the hired guns could have worn gloves.

It was time to move on to a question that Levi had to ask, but he dreaded hearing the answer.

"Has it gotten around yet that I'm claiming the baby is Alexa's and mine?"

"Oh, yeah. I'm guessing the medic blabbed to everyone who'd listen. Or maybe it was Lockwood." Jericho paused. "Mom heard. And Jax."

Great, just great. All of his family was holding a grudge against Alexa, but his brother, Jax, had the biggest reason, since it was his wife who'd been murdered after Alexa had gotten Paige involved in the Moonlight Strangler investigation.

"Do Jax and Mom know the truth yet?" Levi asked.

"They've probably figured it out. If not, I'll fill them in first chance I get. Any ideas, though, as to how I fill them in? How much do I tell them? Or do you want me just to keep lying?"

Lying was the last route Levi wanted to take with this. Not where his family was concerned. Still, the truth could increase the danger. "That depends on what we learn in the next few hours. Please tell me you found something to pin this on Lockwood or anyone else."

"No. Sorry. But here's what I do know. Most of Lockwood's fellow marshals think he's an SOB. After talking with him, I agree. But while no one, including me, likes him much, there's no proof he's dirty or responsible for those attacks last night."

"Then who is responsible?" Levi snapped out of frustration.

"My magic crystal ball is a little cloudy this morning, but Marcos always turns up when something dirty's going down."

True. It was hard to get dirtier than Marcos. "Any chance Marcos is pulling Lockwood's strings?"

"Maybe. Marcos wants Alexa dead so she can't testify against him next month, and I think anyone after Alexa is just doing Marcos's bidding."

That's what Levi thought, too. "Is there any way we can try to put a leash on Lockwood in case he's Marcos's henchman?"

"I'm working on it. But I'm keeping Chase out of it for a least a little while, agreed?"

"Agreed."

His brother, Chase, was a marshal, but he was also recovering from an attack that'd happened just a few weeks earlier. Chase hadn't been cleared for duty, and Levi didn't want to put any of this on Chase's shoulders. Besides, this had another personal connection for Chase. The woman carrying his baby, April Landis, was also in WITSEC and would testify against another criminal connected to Marcos's illegal activities.

"Is there another marshal who can help us?" Levi asked.

"Dallas Walker," Jericho answered without hesitating. "He's agreed to keep eyes on Lockwood to make sure he doesn't try to harass Alexa again."

That was a good start. "What about Lockwood's threat to force Alexa back into his custody?" But the question sort of died on his lips when Alexa came out of the bathroom.

She was dressed, her hair damp from the shower, and she was wearing jeans and a white shirt she'd gotten from the closet. The clothes were too big for her, concealing her body, yet somehow not concealing it at all. The shirt skimmed in all the wrong places. Wrong because Levi noticed.

Something he shouldn't have been doing.

"What about Lockwood's threat?" she repeated, moving closer to him.

Levi caught her scent. Not just the soap from the shower but something else beneath it. He knew because he'd used the same soap about an hour earlier, and it darn sure didn't smell like that on him.

"Alexa's awake," Jericho said. Obviously, he'd heard her voice. "Put the call on speaker then so she can listen."

Levi did, but he moved to the other side of the room so they wouldn't wake the baby. Of course, as small as the place was, the baby would probably be able to hear them anyway, but Jericho had a tendency to curse. A lot. And even though Violet was way too young to understand the words, she might still pick up on the mood. Now that his brother would be talking to Alexa, Levi figured that mood was going to get a lot darker than it already was.

"Marshal Walker doesn't believe there are grounds for Lockwood to force her back into his custody," Jericho explained. "Unless Lockwood can come up with proof that she did hack into WITSEC files."

"There's no proof because I didn't do it," Alexa insisted.

"I believe you," Jericho said, surprising both Levi and her. "Lockwood claims you did the hacking to find the Moonlight Strangler. *Really*? Now, while I believe you'd commit a felony or two to find that particular killer, I doubt you'd go about it this way. It's too inefficient."

It wasn't a resounding endorsement of Alexa, but Levi was glad Jericho was on their side about this.

Levi frowned.

Since when had this become *their* side?

Man, he really needed to put some distance between Alexa and him. And that was his next step.

"Until Lockwood's cleared of any suspicion,

I think we all agree it's not safe to turn Alexa over to the marshals," Levi said, speaking to both Jericho and her. "But she and the baby need protection."

"You volunteering to do that?" Jericho asked.

Levi opened his mouth to give a quick *no*. He wasn't volunteering, but someone needed to do protection details. Not Jericho. He was too busy with the investigation and the other cases he was already handling.

Jax was out, too, because of Paige's connection to Alexa.

That left the deputies. Experienced, yes, but it wasn't as if they didn't have full plates with this investigation and others. In fact, the heavy workload was one of the reasons Jericho had jumped to offer Levi a deputy position after he'd left the SAPD.

"Alexa and the baby will need a safe house," Levi finally said to Jericho. "And bodyguards who are used to dealing with newborns. That'll free me up to help you find whoever put them in danger."

Jericho made a sound of agreement. "I'll get started on that. And I'll call when I hear anything about Lockwood or all the other rattlesnakes in this woodpile," Jericho added before ending the call.

Levi wasn't usually a glass-half-empty kind

of guy, but nothing about this situation was ideal or even going his way. Well, except for the fact Alexa, Violet and he were all still alive.

Alexa had a look at the baby and then helped herself to a cup of coffee. She made the same grimace Levi was sure he'd made, and like him, she took another sip.

And she stared at him.

Probably waiting to see what, if anything, he was going to volunteer. Maybe bracing herself for the worst, as well. Too bad she had to look so dang hot while doing that.

What was wrong with him?

His head was already a mess what with everything else going in his life. He definitely didn't need to add Alexa to the mix.

"I know you're eager to get me out of your hair." She glanced at the bedroom. "Out of your bed, too." Almost immediately her eyes widened, and she actually blushed. "Sorry. I didn't mean it that way. I just know you'd rather have someone else, anyone else, guarding me."

Levi waved it off. Maybe he wasn't the only one feeling these weird, unwanted vibes. Another glance at Alexa and he got verification of that. Her gaze slid over him, slowly, before she mumbled something he didn't catch and looked away.

"Any news on Tasha?" she asked.

Levi didn't know which of them seemed more relieved to be moving on to something that didn't involve long, lingering looks. And thoughts about the way she smelled. Unfortunately, he didn't have much in the way of helping this conversation along.

"Nothing. The CSIs are still at the scene, though. They found some blood. Also found that someone had tried to wash the blood away. Something else might turn up, though."

She eased down in the chair across from him. "Why wasn't Tasha's body at that gas station?" Her voice cracked. So did the thin composure, and the tears threatened again.

"Only two explanations as to why she wasn't there." Levi had given this plenty of thought. "Either someone moved her or she moved herself."

"Tasha didn't move herself. I saw that man shoot her in the head. I saw her fall."

"You're sure?" And Levi saw the hurt flash through her eyes. "No, I'm not accusing you of lying. It's just I've seen another death the marshals faked for someone going into WITSEC and it was pretty realistic. What if Tasha set all this up so she could disappear for good, and she could have done that to get away from Scottie?"

Alexa was shaking her head before he even

finished. "She wouldn't have left Violet behind. She loves her baby."

Levi couldn't imagine her leaving Violet, either, but there was another possibility when it came to Tasha. "Maybe she's not planning on leaving the baby permanently. Maybe when she's regrouped, Tasha will come for her."

More head shaking from Alexa. "Tasha wouldn't have put Violet in danger like that."

"It's possible she didn't have a choice."

He glanced at the baby when Violet made a whimpering sound. Both Alexa and he reached for the laundry basket to give it a gentle rock. Unlike the other times he'd tried it throughout the night, it actually worked. Violet went back to sleep.

"A choice," Alexa repeated, automatically lowering her voice to a whisper. "You mean because she knew Scottie had learned where she was?"

"Or she could have known he would eventually find her. Are you sure the men were using real bullets when they shot at Tasha and you?" he asked.

"Yes," she snapped. Then she groaned softly. "No. I can't be positive. But I did see some blood. Which could have been faked, I suppose. However, those gunmen shot real bullets at us after we left the Outlaw Bar. And I won't ever believe

Tasha ordered someone to do that, especially not with Violet in the car with us."

Levi couldn't see a mother doing that to a child, but the truth was mothers did bad things all the time. "How well did you know Tasha?" he asked.

Alexa frowned, obviously not pleased with the direction of this conversation. Still, she didn't just blow it off. "We got close over the past couple months." She glanced away. "I did a thorough background search on her, and she didn't have a criminal record. Before you read too much into that, I ran background checks on everyone who came in contact with me. I wanted to make sure Marcos wasn't trying to slip someone into my very small circle of friends and acquaintances."

Understandable. Levi would have done the same thing. And that was exactly the sort of thing Marcos would try to pull. "Any red flags when it came to Tasha?"

Alexa looked as if she wanted to say no, but that wasn't her answer. "Maybe. Not red flags to connect her to Marcos, but she did work for a loan shark for a while. Again, nothing criminal on her part. She worked as a secretary for the investment business he was using as a front for his illegal activity. When she found out what he was doing, she quit."

Levi didn't like the sound of that. Even if she'd

quit, that didn't mean her ex-boss would just let her walk.

"You remember the loan shark's name?" Levi asked.

She nodded. "Nick Perryman. But you don't think he has anything to do with this, do you?"

"Only way to know is to check him out." He paused. "Tasha really doesn't have a next of kin?"

"No. Her parents were killed when she was a teenager and she was raised in foster care after that." Alexa glanced at the baby again, sighed. "Of course, Violet's father might have relatives who'd want her. Like I told you, Tasha said his name was Brett Mendoza, and she also said she had amnio results to prove it."

"Amnio?" Levi questioned. He'd heard the term but had no idea what it meant.

"It's a test that pregnant women sometimes have to make sure there's nothing wrong. Tasha had had some kind of infection early in the pregnancy, and the doctors did the test to rule out medical problems. But the results also confirmed both the sex and the paternity of the baby."

"She had a sample of Mendoza's DNA to compare?"

"I guess so because she said it was a match. I'm not sure though where Tasha put the test results."

They were probably still at her place in Austin. Levi could maybe get a search warrant, and if that didn't turn up anything, he could possibly get the results from her doctor.

Well, once the woman's death was confirmed, that is.

"Tasha must have had doubts about the baby's paternity," Levi continued, "if she had the DNA confirmed during that test."

"Maybe. The test wasn't for paternity though. It was for medical reasons, but I guess Tasha must have gotten the results anyway."

That was possible, but Levi still wanted to verify it if he could. He texted Brett Mendoza's and Perryman's names to Mack and asked him to do a quick check on the men. According to Tasha, Mendoza was dead, but he wasn't sure everything Tasha had said and done was the truth.

"How long was it between the time you left the gas station and met me at the Outlaw Bar?" he asked.

"Less than an hour."

That's what he'd estimated, too. "And it was less than a half hour for Dexter to make it out to the gas station to look for the bodies. That's not much time for the second gunman to do a cleanup and move two bodies. Unless he had plenty of help," Levi added.

Alexa paused, clearly processing what he was saying, but then she shook her head again.

However, before she could explain why she still wasn't buying the possibility of a faked death scene, Levi's phone buzzed. Despite the fact he had the sound turned down, Violet must have heard it because she started to cry.

"It's Teddy McQueen, one of the ranch hands," Levi relayed to Alexa as she put her coffee aside and scooped up the baby.

While Levi wanted to believe Teddy was calling about some ranch business, that hope vanished when he heard Teddy's voice. Since any and all bad news was likely connected to Alexa, he put the call on speaker.

"Some guy just showed up on the road leading to the main house," Teddy said. "He's only about thirty yards from the guesthouse and he's already spotted the police cruiser, so I guess he knows you're here. We're not letting him get any closer, but he's demanding to talk to you."

Levi definitely didn't like the timing of any visitor. "Who is he?"

"He won't give us a name, but he's a big fella. About six foot three with light brown hair."

Alexa made a soft, strangled sound. "It could be Scottie Norse," she whispered, and Levi had no trouble hearing something in her voice, too.

The fear.

"Take a picture of this man and text it to me," Levi instructed. "Did he say what he wanted?"

"Yeah, he did. He said he wanted to make some kind of exchange."

Levi didn't like the sound of that. "What kind of exchange?" he asked Teddy.

"He says if you tell him where he can find some woman named Tasha and her kid, then he'll tell you how to find the Moonlight Strangler."

Chapter Six

Alexa rocked Violet and held her breath. She was waiting for the photo that Teddy had taken of their visitor to load on Levi's phone.

She'd only seen one photo of Scottie, and according to Tasha, it'd been taken several years earlier when Tasha was still dating the man. However, unless Scottie had altered his appearance, Alexa thought she'd still be able to recognize him.

And she did.

It felt like a punch to the stomach when Scottie's face appeared on the phone screen. No altered appearance. He looked the same as he had in that picture, with one exception. He was actually smiling in the shot Teddy had taken of him. Considering he was a brute, a stalker and possibly a killer, that smile chilled Alexa to the bone.

"It's Scottie," she verified.

Levi drew in a long breath. "You know if he

has any connection whatsoever to the Moonlight Strangler?"

She had to shake her head. "Nothing's come up in my investigation. Anything in yours?"

Levi shook his head, as well. Which meant Scottie could be using this as some kind of ruse to draw them out. Because of his abusive history with Tasha, the man had to know that Levi wouldn't just tell him where she was.

"If he's asking for Tasha's whereabouts, he must not think she's dead." Levi paused. "But he's also asking about the baby, so maybe it's Violet he really wants now that Tasha's dead?"

That caused Alexa to hold the baby even closer. "He's not getting anywhere near her."

"Agreed."

Good. Not that she'd thought for one second Levi would give in to Scottie's demands. Levi and she might be at odds because of Paige's death, but they were on the same side when it came to protecting the baby.

"Well?" she heard someone call out. Not Teddy's voice this time. Probably Scottie's. "Deputy, do we have a deal? Info about the Moonlight Strangler in exchange for info about Tasha and the baby. I love Tasha and I have to talk to her. I want to make her understand that I can love her baby, too. I just need to find out where they are."

Since Violet was still whimpering, Alexa gave her a pacifier. It was something she'd seen Tasha do, and thankfully this time it worked. "If Scottie's the one who killed Tasha, then why would he still want to know where the baby is?" Alexa whispered.

"No good reason I can think of. Maybe this is his sick way of trying to hold on to a piece of Tasha. Or maybe he wasn't the one who killed her."

Yes, because maybe Tasha wasn't dead after all. Or maybe she'd been the victim of some thug Marcos had hired. Too bad Alexa was certain that Scottie wouldn't, or couldn't, tell them the truth about what'd really happened at the gas station.

"Stay out of sight and keep quiet," Levi mouthed to her, and he started for the front door.

"You can't go out there," she insisted. "He could be the one trying to kill us."

Not that Levi had to be reminded of that. But Alexa was talking to the air because he was indeed already heading outside. Levi ended the call with Teddy and put his phone back in his jeans pocket. No doubt so that his hands would be free to draw his gun if it became necessary.

"Who's Tasha?" Levi called out. "And what do you know about the Moonlight Strangler?"

It didn't surprise her that Levi pretended not to know Tasha. No need to give Scottie any information.

But how had Scottie even guessed that Tasha might be there?

Since his money and connections had kept him out of jail, Scottie might have used those same connections to learn about the attack at the gas station. Maybe even her trip to the Appaloosa Pass sheriff's office.

"Let's not play games, Deputy Crockett," Scottie answered. "You know who and where she is."

There were only two windows at the front of the guesthouse, and Alexa went to the one in the kitchen area so she could peek out the side of the blinds. She didn't move the curtain, didn't lift the blind slat because she didn't want Scottie to see that anyone else was inside.

And there he was.

Standing next to a flame-red sports car, Scottie was an imposing man in a tan coat. A coat that could conceal a weapon. However, there was a ranch hand on each side of him, and she saw that Levi, too, had already drawn his gun.

"If Tasha wasn't here, you wouldn't be having this kind of security," Scottie said, tipping his head to the armed hands.

"As I'm sure you know, my family has *connections* to the Moonlight Strangler. The security measures are to keep him out along with anyone else who wants to break the law."

Scottie smiled again. "Oh, I see. You believe Tasha's side. I didn't assault her, you know. An argument just got out of hand, and rather than admit she was wrong, she had me arrested and then she took off. I want to find her."

"I want a lot of things," Levi countered. "Like a quick end to this conversation before I freeze my butt off out here. If you know anything about the Moonlight Strangler, then spill it now, or I'll have you arrested for obstruction of justice."

If that threat bothered Scottie, it didn't show on his face. "I'm willing to cooperate, to share with you what I know. But I have to find Tasha. I believe she and her baby are in grave danger."

"From you," Levi snapped.

Now, that bothered Scottie. Even at this distance and from her limited view, she could see his face go hard. "I wouldn't hurt her. Wouldn't hurt her baby, either. But the baby's father might not feel the same as I do. It's a guy named Brett Mendoza. A real lowlife. I think he wants to hurt Tasha because she left him. He might take his anger out on the baby."

Scottie might feel the same way about hurting the baby. A thought that sickened her.

"I'll be wanting any information you have about Mendoza, too," Levi added quickly.

Scottie cursed. No more smiling, nice guy facade. The dangerous thug emerged. "I need to find Tasha now!" he yelled.

"Send whatever you have about the Moonlight Strangler and Mendoza to the Appaloosa Pass sheriff's office. Once I've read the info, we'll talk."

"Is Tasha with that bitch PI who's been visiting her?" Scottie's shout seemed to echo through the house.

Levi had already turned to come back inside, but that stopped him. "What PI?" he asked, his tone sounding even more dangerous than their visitor's.

"You damn well know, and one way or another I will find them."

"Just get that info to the sheriff's office," Levi warned him. "By the way, where were you last night?"

"Why?" Scottie snapped.

Levi tapped his badge, repeated his question and waited for what would probably be either a well-crafted lie or more likely a well-crafted alibi that Scottie had put in place so he couldn't be connected to the attacks.

"I was working," Scottie finally said. "At the Norse building in downtown San Antonio. And no, it's not a coincidence that the building has my surname. My father owns it and I work for him."

Of course. What else? A loose cannon like Scottie probably couldn't get a job any other way.

"How late were you there?" Levi continued.

"*Late*. There are security cameras that monitor who comes and goes. Get a court order and check them out if you don't believe me."

"Oh, I will," Levi assured him. "I'll check out a lot of things and find something I can use to arrest you if you don't give me what you have on the Moonlight Strangler and Mendoza."

Scottie belted out more profanity, got back in his car and sped away.

Levi didn't linger out there, either. "Call me if he comes back," he told the hands, and when he stepped back inside his attention went straight to Alexa. "You okay?"

It took her a moment to realize why he'd asked that. She was shaking, and it wasn't from the drop in temperature at having the door open for those several minutes while Levi had been talking with Scottie.

What had shaken her were the things Scottie had said.

"Scottie must not have killed Tasha since he's still looking for her." Alexa had some trouble getting that out. Had even more trouble trying to deal with it.

Because it put Tasha's death back on her.

"If Scottie didn't kill Tasha, then she died

because of me," she spelled out. "I got another woman killed." Her voice was all breath now, and Levi locked the door and hurried to her. Probably because she looked ready to collapse.

He took the baby from her, eased Violet back into the basket and then gripped Alexa's arm, forcing her to sit down.

"Will this ever end?" The sob came before she could stop it. So did the tears.

Levi went to his knees in front of her, and much to her surprise—probably to his surprise, too—he pulled her into his arms. He didn't say anything right away. He just held her. And Alexa got another surprise when she realized just how comforting his arms could be. All that warmth. All that strength.

Alexa couldn't help herself. She leaned in closer, taking something she knew Levi would later regret. She would, too, because getting close to him was a really bad idea. Unfortunately, with his arms around her, she was having trouble remembering exactly why it was bad.

Levi must have remembered, though, because he pulled back and his gaze met hers. She saw the "oh, no" look in his eyes. Alexa knew exactly how he felt. Any involvement with Levi would end badly, and she didn't have the emotional energy to deal with it.

Even if her body disagreed.

"Scottie could be lying about everything he just told us," Levi said.

Good. It was a reminder she needed along with being a real possibility. After all, Scottie wasn't a good guy, so naturally he was capable of lying.

"Scottie could know that Tasha's dead," Levi went on. "Because he could have been responsible for her death."

Alexa nodded. "And he came here, maybe because he thought it would make him look less guilty if he claimed to know she wasn't dead."

Levi nodded, too. "He probably figured offering me the Moonlight Strangler info would sweeten the pot, but he must have known there was no way I'd reveal the location of Tasha and the baby."

Alexa thought about that a moment. "So maybe Scottie doesn't want the baby after all?"

"That's possible. It's hard to tell what those hired guns wanted last night when they attacked us. That definitely didn't seem like a kidnapping attempt."

She agreed, and that took her back to the theory of two different attacks. One that'd been designed to kill Tasha. That would have been Scottie's doing, of course, but the second one could have been all Marcos. As bad as it was to have two monsters after her, at least it meant she might not have been the reason Tasha was killed.

Levi took out his phone. "I need to call Mack." He put the call on speaker and the deputy answered on the first ring. "Mack, it's a long shot, but you might be getting a visitor. Someone who'll be bringing info about the Moonlight Strangler and Brett Mendoza, the guy I asked you to run a background check on."

"Are those two connected?" Mack asked immediately. "Because I sure didn't find anything to link them."

"Probably not, but Tasha's stalking ex, Scottie Norse, was just here at the ranch, and he claimed to have something. If he has anything at all, I doubt he'll bring it in person, but if he does, watch out. The guy's got a very short fuse."

"Will do."

"I also need to see if we can get a court order for security footage from the Norse building in San Antonio. I suspect Scottie was there as he claims, but I need to verify his alibi."

"I can get started on that," Mack assured him. "I got something on Brett Mendoza and that loan shark, Nick Perryman. They're not full reports yet, but I found enough to know there's a problem. Mendoza's dead all right. Not a car accident, though. His car exploded when he started the engine, and it's being investigated as a homicide."

Sweet heaven. Alexa didn't know Mendoza, but Tasha had cared deeply for him. Plus, he was Violet's father.

"Please tell me Scottie's a suspect," she said.

"Definitely, but he has an ironclad alibi for the day of the blast. Of course, that doesn't mean he couldn't have hired someone to do it. Dallas PD is looking for a paper trail that could lead to Scottie."

A trail she was betting Scottie had hidden well.

"And Perryman?" Levi asked Mack.

"Definitely a loan shark. Nothing to indicate, though, that he was so riled at Tasha that he'd go after her, but SAPD's going to ask around and see if they can dig up anything. I'll call you if I get something." With that Mack hung up.

Alexa wouldn't hold her breath for anything on a connection between Perryman and Tasha. People who ratted on loan sharks didn't have long lives.

"What about the info Scottie claimed he had about the Moonlight Strangler?" Alexa asked Levi.

"Again, it could be a lie. If Scottie doesn't take anything to the sheriff's office, I was serious about those obstruction of justice charges."

That probably wouldn't keep Scottie behind bars for long, but it would be a start. Of course, the man might have actually found something. The Moonlight Strangler had a habit of writing letters to various people. That could have happened even though Alexa wasn't sure how the killer could have crossed paths with Scottie.

"It wouldn't have been hard for Scottie to learn I've been working to find the Moonlight Strangler and that I would want anything anyone had about him," Levi said. He moved away from her and went to the window. Probably to make sure Scottie wasn't returning.

But Alexa also got the feeling it was because he wanted to put some distance between them. He definitely dodged her gaze.

"I want to find the Moonlight Strangler," he added. "I want to avenge Paige's death."

Alexa nodded. "I understand."

That was an understatement, since she blamed herself for what had happened to Paige. But Levi blamed himself, too. He'd been on the task force to catch the Moonlight Strangler, and in his mind he would always believe he had failed.

A failure that had caused his brother's wife to be murdered.

Levi turned, putting his back to her. "SAPD highly encouraged me to leave the force. According to my lieutenant, I'd become obsessed with finding the Moonlight Strangler. I couldn't argue with that. I *am* obsessed with it."

Yes, so was she. And it had probably indeed affected Levi's other cases. It had certainly affected her life. Her judgment, too.

"I swore to Jax that I'd find Paige's killer before the anniversary of her death," Levi continued. "I only have six months left and I'm not any closer to finding him now than I was when Paige was killed."

Not that he'd needed to tell Alexa the timeline. Paige had been murdered the month before Alexa had been forced into WITSEC.

"As you know, I was investigating the Moonlight Strangler before Paige was ever killed. And you know the reason," she said.

Levi nodded. "He killed one of your childhood friends."

"Not just a friend. Trisha Duncan. My best friend. She was like a sister to me."

Another nod. "And you promised her family you'd find him." Levi paused. "Promises are sometimes very hard to keep."

They were, but that didn't mean she would just give up. "Has the Moonlight Strangler contacted your sister, Addie?"

She saw the jaw muscles tighten on the side of his face that was visible to her. Something that usually happened whenever she asked about his family. Levi probably didn't want her to think of anyone in his family as a possible link to the killer.

But the link was already there, and it was a huge one.

His parents had adopted Addie when she was a toddler. Levi's father had been the sheriff at the time and had put Addie's DNA in the databases. Finally, years later, and long after Levi's father had passed away, there'd been a match for Addie's DNA.

Addie's biological father was the "unsub" or unknown subject that the press had dubbed the Moonlight Strangler.

From everything Alexa had heard, the news had caused a firestorm in the Crockett family with Levi and his brothers all scrambling to protect her. Addie's now husband Weston had done the same. But there'd been no threat to her from her birth father. No threat to Addie's biological brother, Cord Granger, either.

"The Moonlight Strangler called Addie a couple of months ago," Levi answered finally. "The conversation's been analyzed six ways to Sunday, and there are no clues as to his identity. He did say, though, that he wouldn't come after Addie, and so far he's kept that promise."

Of course, Levi would trust that promise about as far as he could toss a house. Alexa felt the same way. As long as the Moonlight Strangler was out there, his sister and the rest of his family were in danger.

Ditto for Alexa being in danger as long as Marcos was around.

With the trial still a month away, that meant she'd have to stay in hiding. Alexa also knew there was something else she had to do.

"If Scottie believes Violet is ours, she should be safe," she said. "But it certainly won't protect her from Marcos. He could come after me again, and Violet could get hurt. That means I have to put some distance between her and me."

Levi turned, stared at her. "You heard what I said to Jericho about finding a safe house and someone qualified to guard Violet." He glanced around, no doubt emphasizing the cramped quarters. "We can't stay here much longer, and besides we don't know what we're doing when it comes to taking care of a baby."

Alexa couldn't argue with that last part. Not completely anyway. After multiple tries, she'd finally gotten Violet's diaper to stay on. Levi had dropped the first bottle he'd fixed, but he'd managed to hang on to the second one.

"We both suck at burping," she grumbled. It'd taken her a half hour just to get a tiny burp from Violet. Alexa hadn't meant what she said to be funny, but the corner of Levi's mouth lifted in a smile.

A short-lived one.

"I'll miss her," Alexa went on. "I mean, I haven't been around her that long, but I've gotten attached to her."

"Yeah," Levi agreed. He seemed both surprised and annoyed by that attachment.

"Do you want kids?" she asked. More surprise, this time in his eyes, and after their holding session, it sounded, well, intimate or something. "It wasn't an invitation," Alexa added, causing him to smile again. "I'm just curious."

"One day, yes. I want kids. You? And that also wasn't an invitation."

Except his smile sort of made her feel as though it was. Of course, that was her stupid body's way of seeing it, and it was the wrong way. Levi might feel the same attraction for her that she did for him, but there was no way he'd act on it.

Was there?

Alexa didn't even get a chance to let herself play around with that notion. Levi's phone buzzed, and she saw Jericho's name on the screen. Like the other call from Mack, Levi put it on speaker the moment he answered.

"Did Scottie show up?" Levi asked right off.

"No. Not yet." And Jericho's gloomy tone had Alexa's stomach tightening. "But I do have news. You should probably come on in to work since I have Marcos in an interview room."

"Marcos?" Levi and she asked in unison. It was Levi who continued. "Why is he there?"

"Because he's a suspect in what has now become a murder investigation." Jericho paused. "Levi, we've found two bodies."

Chapter Seven

"Where's Marcos?" Levi asked the moment he and Alexa stepped into the sheriff's office.

"Interview room," Jericho answered, tipping his head to the far end of the hall. "Come on. Let's go in my office. That way if Marcos or his lawyer comes out, they won't see Alexa or the baby."

It was a good plan. Well, not good exactly. Nothing about this fell into the good category.

Of course, Levi hadn't wanted Alexa or Violet anywhere near Marcos, but he hadn't exactly had a lot of options about bringing them into town. Jericho had wanted Alexa to view the live feed the medical examiner would be sending so she could possibly confirm if the two DBs had any part in the attacks. Plus, she still needed to give them statements for their investigation.

Levi had debated leaving Alexa and the baby with the ranch hands while he came to the office to view both the ME's feed and do those reports. However, considering that Scottie could still be around and might be watching the ranch, Levi hadn't wanted Scottie to make a return visit.

That meant Levi had brought Alexa and Violet along with him.

Normally Levi would have considered the sheriff's office a safe place, but with a possible killer under the same roof, no place was safe. Especially not for Alexa and the baby. He'd soon have Violet's safety remedied, though, because the protection detail would arrive shortly to whisk her off to a safe house.

It was the right thing to do.

Levi knew that in his head, but for some reason he hated the notion of handing her off to people she didn't know. Of course, just hours earlier Violet hadn't known him, but still it stung. The only thing that was making this palatable was he was certain it was their only option for keeping the baby safe.

Once they were in Jericho's office he shut the door, locked it and turned the computer screen in their direction. It only took a few key strokes before the images of a dead body appeared on the screen.

Not Tasha as Levi had first thought it would be.

This was a man. A stranger. But judging

from the gasping sound Alexa made, he wasn't a stranger to her.

"That's the man I hit with the flashlight," she said. "The one who came after Tasha and me at the gas station."

Since Alexa looked a little unsteady while she still had Violet in her arms, Levi helped her into one of the chairs by Jericho's desk. Jericho went a step further and took the baby from her, easing Violet into a carrier seat that he had brought over from the hospital.

"Show us the next body," Jericho instructed the ME.

Levi put his hand on Alexa's shoulder, hoping it would help brace her for the worst—seeing Tasha's dead body.

But again it wasn't Tasha.

It was another man.

Alexa's breath came out in a rush and she nearly went limp with relief. "That's the second man who attacked us."

"Yeah, that's what I figured. We got immediate hits on both sets of fingerprints," Jericho explained. "Their names are Hector Litton and Charlie Hagerman. Ring any bells?" he asked Alexa.

"No. Who are they?"

"Part-time bouncers and full-time criminals. Judging from their arrest records, they liked to beat up people who owed money to various loan sharks around the area. Both also once worked for Marcos. That's why Marcos is in the interview room with his lawyer right now."

If only Marcos would spill something about this, but Levi doubted they'd get anything remotely resembling a confession from the man.

"Where's Tasha's body?" Alexa asked.

Jericho shook his head. "The CSIs are still searching the area."

So, Tasha could still be alive. Because it didn't make sense to dump her away from Litton and Hagerman. Of course, that led Levi to the big question of who had dumped those two?

"We'll process the bodies and see if there's any trace that'll connect them to Tasha," Jericho explained.

Alexa stared at the screen where she could now see both dead thugs. "So, I did kill that man," she said under her breath.

"Did you shoot him?" Jericho quickly asked.

Alexa met Jericho's stare. "No. I didn't have a gun. I hit him in the head with a flashlight."

Jericho tapped the first man's head on the screen. "Blunt force trauma wasn't the cause of his death. A bullet was. It entered right at the point of the injury you gave him so that's why it's a little hard to see."

Levi hadn't spotted it right off, but after taking another look, he saw it.

"A bullet killed the second guy, too," Jericho went on. "Both point-blank range, and there are no defensive wounds, which means they likely knew their killer."

Alexa looked up at Levi, likely wanting him to come up with a solid reason why this had happened, but he only had theories. Well, one theory anyway that Alexa wasn't going to like.

Levi put his theory out there for her to hear. "If Tasha faked her own death, then she could have hired these two to do the job. And then maybe she killed them so they couldn't be traced back to her."

At least Alexa didn't jump to nix it. Not immediately. But then she glanced at Violet. "Tasha wouldn't have put the baby in danger."

"Maybe she didn't." Levi turned to Jericho when Alexa huffed. "Alexa and I have already discussed the possibility that Tasha used fake bullets and blood to make it look as if she'd been murdered. She could have done that to escape Scottie for good."

"Is Tasha capable of murder?" Jericho asked.

"No," Alexa snapped, but then she shook her head. "Unless she's been playing me for these past months."

"Wouldn't be the first time you were played," Jericho reminded her.

Alexa flinched but couldn't deny it. The Moonlight Strangler had tricked her into meeting him the night he'd murdered Paige. And while that meant Alexa didn't have a good track record in this department, Levi wasn't one hundred percent sure that Tasha was still alive.

"Scottie could have hired those men to kill Tasha, and then Scottie could have killed them," Levi admitted. "He might want everyone to believe Tasha is still alive and that she's a killer. That way he walks for her murder and the attack on Alexa and me."

"Thank you for believing me." Alexa got to her feet, and in the same motion she hugged him. Not something Levi and Jericho had expected.

Jericho scowled first at Alexa and then at Levi when Levi didn't push her away. However, Levi did move Alexa to the crook of his arm so they could continue this conversation face-to-face with his brother.

"Of course, if Scottie was only after Tasha, then that probably means Marcos attacked you," Jericho said. "Or Lockwood. Does Lockwood have a reason to go after you on his own? By that I mean does he have a personal reason for wanting you dead?"

"Yes," Alexa admitted. "When I worked for

Marcos, I saw the names of the people involved in his illegal activities. Most were aliases, and one could have been Lockwood. I don't have anything to prove that, but maybe Lockwood believes with the PI's help that I'm close to connecting the dots. That's why I didn't tell Lockwood the PI's name because I was afraid he might go after him."

"Lockwood would if he's dirty." Jericho moved a writing tablet and pen to the edge of his desk. "Give me the name of the PI. I'll see what I can find out."

Alexa didn't hesitate. She jotted down the name, James Moser. The very PI that Levi had used sometimes when he worked as a San Antonio cop.

Even though Levi knew that Alexa had been in contact with James, he hadn't realized until now that James had also been the source for what Alexa had heard about Lockwood. Of course, James was always on the lookout for ways to earn some extra cash with talk that he heard from his seedier clients and the bar he frequented. The bar was a hangout for all sorts of lowlifes, and James had given Levi plenty of reliable information in the past. Some of it, though, had turned out to be rumors. It was always a challenge to sort out the truth.

"I'll do some checking," Jericho said looking

at the name. He clicked off the computer images. "We'll need to follow up on Scottie and Lockwood. Plus, I'll need to deal with the sociopath up the hall."

Marcos.

"Can I listen in on what he has to say?" Alexa asked.

Levi saw the debate in Jericho's eyes. A quick one. "I'll get Dexter to stay in here with the baby. That way she's not near the interview room. You and Levi can watch Marcos through the observation mirror."

Even though it went against his brother's grain to cooperate with anything having to do with Alexa, it was a wise decision to have her listen. Alexa was a former PI after all, and she knew Marcos. She might be able to pick up on something that Jericho might miss.

Jericho called Dexter, and he didn't open the door until the deputy knocked. "Sorry, but you got babysitting detail," Jericho said to Dexter. He grabbed some pictures of the dead men off his desk. "While you're in here, make some calls and find out what you can about a PI named James Moser. Don't make waves for him and don't connect him in any way to Alexa."

Because that kind of connection could get James killed. Alexa was already on edge, and

Levi wasn't sure she could handle another death associated with her or her investigation.

Levi led Alexa to the observation room, and he immediately spotted Marcos through the mirror. Levi hadn't actually met the man, but he recognized him from his pictures. Early thirties, spiky reddish-brown hair, the kind of style that stood out in a cowboy town. Ditto for the slick silver-gray suit. He looked more like a rock star on the way to an awards ceremony than a criminal on his way to prison. Hopefully.

Marcos was well past the basic criminal stage. Alexa would be testifying against him for money laundering and extortion, but Levi was betting that was just the tip of the iceberg. Too bad the cops hadn't been able to pin something on him that would get him off the streets for the rest of his life. And maybe they could. After all, someone had murdered those two men.

There was another suit seated next to Marcos. His lawyer, no doubt. The man was at least twenty years older than Marcos and was poring over some kind of document in front of him. He was talking in hushed tones to his client, but Marcos had his attention nailed to the mirror.

"Alexa is here, isn't she?" Marcos asked the moment Jericho stepped into the interview room. He didn't wait for Jericho to answer and definitely didn't stop staring at the mirror. "Why doesn't she come in here so we can talk face-to-face? I like her face. I dream of doing…things to it."

And, yeah, that sounded like the threat it probably was. While there was no way the man could see her, Levi felt Alexa's arm tense.

"I hate that he scares me," she whispered.

"You're smart to be scared. Marcos is a dangerous man."

"I'm here," Jericho announced to Marcos, and he flashed a sappy sweet smile that was a little scary. "Guess you'll have to dream of doing things to my face instead."

Marcos angled his cold blue eyes at Jericho, silently dismissing him, but Levi thought Jericho might have managed to tap into just a bit of the temper Marcos was known to have.

Jericho dropped the pictures on the table in front of Marcos. Alexa tensed again, and Levi knew why. The bodies had been cleaned up some in the footage the ME had streamed to them, but these photos were of the bodies as they'd been found.

Bloody.

Levi slipped his arm around Alexa, something he'd been doing a lot lately, and she melted against him. A good fit. Something he shouldn't have noticed. Or felt. But he did.

"Friends of yours?" Jericho asked, tipping his head to the photos.

Marcos spared each a glance. "Former employees. I believe their names are Hector Litton and Charlie Hagerman. Is that why you had me dragged in here?"

Jericho took his time responding. "In part. In part, too, because I just like dragging you places."

There it was. Another flash of Marcos's temper. His eyes narrowed.

"Where were you last night?" Jericho pressed. "And in case you missed the cue of being in an interview room, I want to hear your alibi."

The lawyer leaned in and whispered something in Marcos's ear.

"I was at a party with friends and stayed the entire night," Marcos answered. "My attorney will provide you with a list of names of the half dozen guests and host who can vouch I was there."

"Of course," Alexa muttered. "If he orchestrated the attack, he would have made sure it couldn't be pinned on him."

"That's a pretty darn big alibi. Those two brainless wonders didn't have alibis though." Jericho motioned toward the photos of the dead men. "Reminding you that this is an official interview and that lying will get your butt in even hotter water, convince me those two former employees weren't following your orders last night."

The lawyer leaned in again, no doubt to whisper something else to his client, but Marcos pushed him away, and when he turned back to Jericho, there was a cocky look on Marcos's face. "There's a presumption of innocence in the law, I believe, so if I tell you those men weren't working for me, then it's your job to either believe it or prove otherwise."

Jericho looked just as cocky. "Yeah, I'm working on the proving otherwise part since there's no way I'm buying that you're innocent."

If that bothered Marcos, he didn't show it. "Do I get to play with Alexa now?"

"No, our playtime's not over yet. Tell me about Marshal Elroy Lockwood," Jericho demanded without pausing.

For the first time since the interview started, Marcos seemed surprised. And uncomfortable. "What about him?"

"I asked first," Jericho countered.

Marcos huffed. "I know Lockwood. I was friends with his younger brother back in high school. Why? Is Lockwood accusing me of something, too? Because if he is he's lying. I haven't seen Lockwood or his brother in a long time."

Alexa glanced at Levi, the question in her

eyes—was this for real? Or was Marcos simply trying to get them off Lockwood's trail? Of course, maybe Marcos really didn't know that Lockwood could have been one of the names involved in the money laundering scheme.

"You're sure about that?" Jericho pressed. "Because presumption of innocence doesn't hold water if I've got a credible witness who says you've dealt with Lockwood recently."

Jericho wasn't telling the truth about the credible witness since the info had come from a secondhand source—the PI who'd told Alexa. But Marcos didn't know where Jericho had gotten the info.

Maybe it would stay that way until they could find James and give him the protection he might need if he did indeed have some kind of proof as to this dirty partnership in the money laundering.

"So, are you or have you ever been in business with Lockwood?" Jericho asked.

"No." Marcos smiled, looked straight in the mirror again. "Alexa." He clucked his tongue. "Are you trying to frame me again?"

"I didn't frame him," Alexa spat out. "I found evidence against him, turned it over to the cops. And because of that snake I can never have a normal life."

Levi tightened his grip on her and braced himself for the tears to start.

"Alexa?" Marcos called out. He stood, tried to go closer to the mirror, but Jericho blocked his path. "Come out, come out wherever you are. It's not like you to hide behind a mirror. Or a badge."

"Don't let him goad you," Levi insisted. But if she heard him, she gave no sign of it. She had her attention fixed to Marcos.

"If I'm the bad guy you think I am, then why don't you look me in the eyes when you say it?" Marcos taunted. "I mean, it's not like you won't have to face me in court. You will." His teeth came together for a moment. "And my lawyers will bury you and any of your Crockett lawmen who have ganged up against me."

"That's enough," Jericho warned him.

"Nowhere near enough." Marcos smiled at him. "Must feel like a knife to the gut for Alexa to be sleeping with your brother. It's surprising that she would bring Levi into this since she believes I'm capable of killing. You'd think she'd be worried about her precious pretty cowboy with that shiny new badge."

Alexa bolted before Levi could stop her. "He knows I'm here. And if he tries to attack me then we win because you can arrest him."

"I don't want you in there with him," Levi insisted.

It didn't work. Nothing short of going caveman and throwing her over his shoulder would have stopped her. And he couldn't blame her. Marcos had essentially just called her out.

Alexa threw open the door to the interview room and glared at Marcos. "You have something to say to me?"

The lawyer didn't just lean this time, he got up and moved between Marcos and her. Jericho did some moving, too.

"Not a good idea," Jericho said to Alexa. But then he looked at her. "Of course, if I were in your shoes, I'd want to face him down, too. Maybe give him a good swift kick where it'll hurt the most. But just remember, you'll get plenty of satisfaction from putting him behind bars."

Levi stepped behind her, eased his arm around her waist. Marcos didn't miss the gesture, and it probably confirmed in his mind that Alexa and Levi were indeed sleeping together.

Marcos smiled, glanced at her stomach. "Funny, you don't look as if you just had a baby."

"Looks can be deceiving," she countered. "I just want you to know that you can't intimidate me into backing off."

Marcos made an I-beg-to-differ sound. "The trouble with caring for someone is that the caring makes you vulnerable. Like Levi, for instance. Right now he wants to come at me and beat me to a pulp." Marcos slid his gaze from Jericho to Levi.

Levi forced himself to shrug. "Well, you do talk a lot and that's annoying, but why would I want to beat you up? All I have to do is wait a few weeks and you'll have plenty of inmates who'll do that for me."

Marcos sure didn't shrug. The flash of temper came again. "I won't be railroaded by a bunch of cowboy cops and her." He jabbed his index finger at Alexa. "So help me, you'll all pay for this."

"How exactly will you do that?" Levi asked calmly.

Now it was Levi who was on the end of Marcos's finger jab. "You'll soon find out. Do you think I'll just let this slide?" His voice got louder with each word. "Do you think there won't be payback?"

Levi wanted to move Alexa out of the way, but she held her ground even when Marcos started toward her. He didn't get far, and this time it wasn't Jericho who intervened. It was the lawyer. He latched on to his client's arm.

"We should be going *now*," the lawyer warned Marcos. The man looked at Jericho. "Call me if you're filing new charges against my client."

Marcos obviously wanted to hold his ground, but the lawyer was persistent and finally got him moving toward the front door. Levi didn't do anything to slow them down because he wanted Marcos far away from Alexa and Violet. Of course, because of the upcoming trial he couldn't keep Marcos away from Alexa forever, but at the moment he wished he could do just that.

Great.

Now he was feeling protective of her. Not a good combination with the attraction. And worse, Levi figured it was only a matter of time before Alexa, he or both of them acted on that attraction.

Marcos shot them all one last glare before his lawyer manhandled him out of the door. As soon as they were outside, Marcos threw off the lawyer's grip with far more force than necessary. And then Marcos punched him.

"Look, he's having a temper tantrum," Jericho joked.

The lawyer rubbed his jaw, dodged another punch and wrestled Marcos into the limo waiting just outside the door. Too bad Marcos hadn't let that temper fly and assaulted Levi. But Levi figured there was no way the lawyer would have let that happen.

"Are you okay?" Levi asked Alexa.

She nodded. But it was a lie. Alexa was shaken and rightfully so. Marcos had just threatened all of them, and the threat wasn't over unless they could figure out how to tie Marcos to the recent attacks.

"I'll check on Violet," she said, turning in that direction.

However, she didn't get far before the front door opened again. Levi automatically drew his gun in case Marcos had decided to act on his threat right here, right now.

But it wasn't Marcos.

It was Scottie.

Scottie didn't have a weapon visible, but he was still wearing that bulky coat. He also had an envelope in his left hand.

Levi so wasn't in the mood to deal with another fool right now, but he had asked Scottie to bring in the so-called evidence he claimed to have. Still, the timing sucked.

"Wait in Jericho's office," Levi told Alexa.

But Scottie had already gotten a good look at her. His expression was pleasant enough. Until it landed on Alexa.

"The lady PI," Scottie said, and it wasn't a friendly greeting. "Finally we meet."

"Former PI," Alexa clarified. She sounded a lot steadier than Levi knew she was. "What did you do to Tasha?"

Scottie held up his hands. "Nothing. I'm here to find out what *you* did to her. Did you convince Tasha to hide from me?" He didn't give Alexa even a second to answer before he continued, "If so, tell me where she is."

Levi had heard more than enough. He holstered his gun and went closer to Scottie so he could frisk him. No gun. Of course, Scottie could have left it in his car since he must have known he'd be searched.

"This isn't a good time to test my patience," Levi warned him. "Now, unless you've got something for me, then you're about to be under arrest for withholding evidence, obstruction of justice, trespassing at the ranch and any other charge I can come up with."

That got Scottie's glare off Alexa and on Levi. Good. Now, maybe she'd go into the office with the baby so he could finish up with Scottie.

"You have no grounds to arrest me," Scottie said once he got his jaw unclenched. "There's the evidence I have regarding the Moonlight Strangler. But if you want to file those charges, you should look at the woman cowering behind you."

Levi wanted to groan. Or punch the guy. "And why would I arrest her?"

Scottie smiled. "Because this evidence belongs to Alexa."

Chapter Eight

Alexa just stared at Scottie, waiting for an explanation about that stupid accusation. But Scottie only handed the envelope to Levi.

"I don't have any evidence connected to the Moonlight Strangler," Alexa insisted, and she repeated it after she turned to Levi.

No matter what was in that envelope, Levi had to believe her. He was just starting to trust her again, and she didn't want to lose what little ground she'd gained with him. She didn't want to lose *him*.

Not that he was hers to lose.

But he certainly wouldn't be offering her his shoulder or his arms if he thought she had kept information about the Moonlight Strangler from him.

She hurried to Levi to get a better look. Jericho made his way there, too. It was a plain white envelope and it was addressed to her or rather to her WITSEC identity. It'd been sent to the house that the marshals had arranged for her. The house where she'd never actually stayed.

"I've never seen that before," she insisted. Then she snapped toward Scottie. "How'd you get it?"

Scottie ignored her question and kept his attention on Levi. "Look inside," Scottie instructed.

The envelope had already been opened, and it had no return address or postmark on it.

"What is this?" Levi asked. "And you can also answer Alexa's question about how you got it."

"Just look inside," Scottie repeated. "Read it and then we can talk about that deal you promised me. Tasha's whereabouts in exchange for information about the Moonlight Strangler."

Levi shook his head. "The only deal I promised you is that I'd arrest you if you withheld evidence."

Scottie clearly didn't like that, but he motioned for Levi to take out the letter. Both Jericho and Alexa leaned in so they could read it. It was short, just a single typed paragraph. Her attention zoomed to the bottom where she saw the sender's name.

The Moonlight Strangler.

"'Alexa-girl'," Levi read aloud. The killer, if this was indeed from the killer, had used her real name instead of the aliases she'd used while in WITSEC. "'You're a hard person to find. Bet you're sleeping with one eye open, huh?'"

She did. And not solely because of the Moonlight Strangler. She had another bogeyman, Marcos, that she had to watch even more.

"'You don't have to be scared of me,'" Levi continued to read. "'I've decided I don't want you dead after all. Better for you to stay alive so you can keep beating yourself up about your friend's death. I do so love watching a girl in misery. If you want to talk about it, go to the Starry, Starry Night website and log in to the chat room. That's where you'll find me. Limited time only, though. Hurry.'"

Levi studied the words a moment longer before he looked at her. "You've never seen this." It wasn't a question, and his gaze slashed to Scottie. "Because I'm guessing you stole it."

Scottie shrugged. "Not really. It was on her porch, and I was going to put it the mailbox, but then the letter fell out."

"What a crock," Levi concluded. "You stole it, opened it and read it. When did all of that happen?"

Jericho didn't wait around to see if Scottie was going to add to that lie. He said something about checking out the website and he went to one of the desks to use a computer.

"Day before yesterday," Scottie admitted, though he didn't seem the least bit concerned that he'd withheld possibly critical evidence for hours. Alexa hoped the killer was still checking into that chat room so Jericho could try to contact him.

And find him.

Of course, she doubted the Moonlight Strangler would just give her his location, but he might let something slip. That was a big *might,* but mights were the only thing they had when it came to the killer.

"How did you find me?" Alexa asked. "How did you find the house where I was supposed to be staying?"

Scottie froze. For just a second. "I didn't find you, exactly. But rather I found Tasha. I knew she was about to deliver the baby, so I got in touch with hospitals, looking for someone who matched her description."

"I'm betting that involved hackers," Alexa said, and she filled in the blanks. "So, you managed to locate Tasha, saw me with her and then what? You didn't follow me to the house, because I didn't go there."

"No, but I got some photos of you. Asked around the area, and when I learned your name, or rather your fake name, I got your address, went to the house to talk to you. That's when I found the letter."

"When you saw that the letter was from the Moonlight Strangler, why didn't you turn it over to the cops?" Levi asked.

"It slipped my mind." Scottie lifted his chin, a defiant pose challenging Levi to argue with that.

"Arrest him," Levi told Mack.

And Mack moved to do exactly that. He holstered his gun and took out some handcuffs.

"What?" Scottie howled. "This is absurd, an abuse of power. Why the hell are you arresting me?"

"Theft and withholding evidence," Levi quickly supplied.

Scottie's face tightened so much it turned red. "You can't do this!"

"Already doing it," Mack assured him.

"Are you even trying to find Tasha?" Scottie snarled while Mack slapped some handcuffs on him. "Mendoza could have—"

"He's dead," Levi interrupted.

Scottie made a flustered sound. "That loan shark then, Perryman."

That got Alexa's attention. "What do you know about him?"

"That he's a bad man capable of doing bad things. You should be arresting him, not me."

Levi shook his head. "I don't have probable

cause to arrest him. Can't say the same for you, though." He motioned for Mack to get moving.

"I demand a phone call." Scottie was still shouting when Mack led him away toward lockup. "That's the law and you can't deny me. I want to call my lawyers. So help me God, I'll have all your badges."

"Good luck with that," Levi said before looking at Mack. "Read him his rights and let him make his one phone call."

That meant Scottie's lawyers would be there in no time. Probably less than an hour. Still, for that hour Scottie wouldn't be out planning another attack.

"Did you find the chat room?" Levi asked. Both Alexa and he went to the desk where Jericho had his attention fixed on the computer screen.

"It's cyberspace for sickos." Jericho turned the laptop screen so they could see it.

Alexa only had to read the first post to realize what Jericho had said was true. The poster who identified himself as ColdMan was looking to buy a corpse.

She cringed. "I'm surprised the site hasn't already been shut down."

"It will be," Jericho assured her. "But I just sent a message to the FBI to ask them to monitor it and check through the old messages to see if there's anything about the Moonlight Strangler. Nothing obvious stands out to me."

Alexa thought about that a moment. "Maybe he wanted me to post something first. If so, he could be checking it."

Jericho nodded. "I'll let the FBI take the lead on this. They can create your online identity and do the post."

Alexa nearly asked him to nix that idea so she could do the post herself. Catching the Moonlight Strangler was her obsession. Or at least it had been. But right now she had so much going on, and the FBI would probably do a better job making contact.

"All right," she finally said, and she didn't think it was her imagination that Jericho and Levi were surprised by that. "I'll check on Violet."

Levi followed her, and Alexa got the feeling he did that to check on her. Probably because once again she looked ready to lose it. And she was. As much as she wanted to catch the Moonlight Strangler, she didn't want that monster coming after her. Especially since she now had Violet.

They were still a few steps from the office door when Levi's phone buzzed. Because most calls he'd gotten had been bad news, Alexa figured the trend would continue. But it was his mother's name, Iris, that appeared on the screen.

"The ranch," he said, quickly jabbing the answer button.

Her heart jumped to her throat, and Alexa prayed her attackers hadn't come to the ranch looking for her. Or worse. That the Moonlight Strangler was there.

"What's wrong?" Levi greeted. Since he didn't put the call on speaker, Alexa moved closer so she could hear.

His mother, however, didn't answer right away. "Is it true?" Iris finally asked. "Is that baby really your daughter that you had with Alexa?"

Even though it wasn't the nightmare Alexa believed that had prompted this call, it was still a tough question. No doubt debating his answer, Levi looked at her. That was when Alexa realized that she was much too close. Levi must have realized it, too, because he put the call on speaker and she stepped back.

"No," he answered. "The baby's not mine."

So, he'd gone with the truth. The only real reason to keep up the lie was to give them time to find out if Violet had a next of kin and to prevent Scottie from trying to hurt or take her. Still, Alexa felt the little tug at her heart.

And silently cursed herself.

Yes, she was definitely losing it. Like Levi,

Violet wasn't hers, and she had to stop thinking of the baby that way.

"I see," Iris said.

"You sound disappointed," Levi pointed out. Alexa agreed.

"Not really. I'd just hoped that you'd found something more fulfilling than the badge and this thirst you have for justice. Don't get me wrong. I want Paige's killer caught, but justice won't bring her back."

"I know that."

This conversation seemed much too personal for Alexa to be hearing, so she stepped away, thinking that Levi would take the call off speaker.

He didn't.

"Do you really know that?" Iris challenged. "Because from what I can tell, you've been living like a monk and working like a dog. Not a good combination, and you deserve more. Of course, I'd rather that *more* not be with Alexa."

Alexa hadn't expected his mother to feel any other way. The Crocketts would always see her as the woman who'd gotten Paige killed, and it didn't matter that Jax and Paige had gotten a divorce shortly before the fateful night of Paige's death. Nothing would change their feelings for Alexa, and even though she had known that, she'd let her guard down. Had let herself feel something she should never have felt when it came to the Crocketts.

Hope that someday they would forgive her.

Hard to do when she couldn't forgive herself.

"Mom, I have to go. I'll phone you when I can." Levi ended the call, and in the same motion he opened the door.

Violet was still asleep in her infant carrier, and the corner of her mouth lifted in a half smile. Just like that Alexa's dark mood lifted. How could she possibly have this reaction, this much love, for a baby who hadn't been in her life just a few days ago?

"Everything okay?" Dexter asked. "I heard lots of yelling going on out there."

"We arrested Scottie," Levi answered.

Dexter nodded in approval. "And Marcos?"

"No grounds to hold him, but he's out of the building." Levi glanced at some notes Dexter had written. "Anything yet on James Moser?"

"Some. I contacted a detective friend at SAPD, and he's going to James's place to talk to him about Lockwood. I didn't mention anything to him about Alexa, but I did tell him to make sure James got police protection if he wants it."

Good. But by now James had likely heard about the attacks the night before, and the PI would put one and one together. James would know that all of this was related to Alexa.

"I could call James," Alexa suggested.

"No way." Levi didn't hesitate, either. "Someone could have tapped his phone. I don't want you to have any contact with the man until we get all of this sorted out."

Before Alexa could say anything else, she heard the voices in the squad room. Definitely not Mack or Jericho, and for a moment she thought Scottie's attorneys had already arrived. However, when Levi opened the door, she saw the two men and a woman. Alexa didn't recognize the woman, but she knew both men. One, Marshal Dallas Walker, wasn't a surprise. But the other was.

Because it was Marshal Chase Crockett.

Jericho didn't look especially pleased about Chase's arrival, but his phone rang, and after glancing at the screen, he stepped aside to take it. "Deal with this," Jericho ordered Levi.

Levi cursed and made a beeline to his brother. "You're supposed to be recovering at home."

"I've recovered," Chase grumbled. "And I wanted to help."

The family resemblance was strong, what with their brown hair and eyes. Similar builds and scowls, too. Scowls they were aiming at each other.

"Is April all right?" Levi asked.

That was another sore subject because it generated another scowl from Chase. "Apparently. If there was a breach in WITSEC, it doesn't seem to have included her."

That was something at least. Both April Landis and Alexa were scheduled to testify against men involved in the money laundering and extortion case. However, Alexa had gotten the better deal in this. She wouldn't be testifying against a cop killer like April would be. Of course, the man April was testifying against was in jail. Unlike Marcos.

Thankfully, Marshal Walker didn't scowl at her. He went to Alexa, hugged her and then glanced into the office at the baby before turning back to Levi.

"I wanted someone on the protection detail I could trust," Dallas explained. "I trust Chase." He lifted his hand to the woman. "This is Patty Dawley, a private bodyguard who specializes in guarding infants and children. I trust her, too."

Levi huffed. "But Chase—"

"Is fine," Chase finished for him. "I would show you that the wound has healed, but I'd prefer not to have to strip off my shirt. I'd rather you take my word for it."

Alexa wanted to do just that, but there must have been doubt all over her face because Chase's next scowl was for her.

"I will protect the baby." Chase stared at her.

"And we really don't have time to stand around here and argue about it. We got a call on the way over. The crime lab found something on the car you drove to the sheriff's office last night."

"The gunmen's vehicle," she said under her breath.

Chase nodded. "A listening device had been hidden in the speakers. You probably don't remember everything Levi and you said when you were in the car, but whoever hired those guns would have heard every word."

Oh, God. Alexa immediately tried to remember their conversation. They'd talked about Lockwood, about how she'd thought he was dirty, but they'd also talked about Violet being Tasha's baby.

"Hell," Jericho said the moment he got off the phone. "Someone called Child Services and they're on their way over to take custody of the baby."

"They can't," Alexa insisted. "They won't be able to protect her if Scottie's goons go after her."

And it didn't matter that Scottie was behind bars at the moment, because he wouldn't be there much longer. Besides, it could take hours or even days to convince a judge that the baby did indeed need protective custody. During that time Violet could be kidnapped or worse.

"They won't take the baby," Jericho assured her. "That's why the protection detail's leaving right now with Violet. She won't be here when the social workers arrive."

Dallas, Chase and the bodyguard all voiced some kind of agreement. Good. It was bending the law to do this, but Alexa knew in her heart that this was the best thing for Violet.

Too bad her heart was also breaking at the thought of having Violet whisked away.

"We're parked out back right by the door," Chase explained. "We need to get out of here."

Alexa knew he was right, but it took Levi's hand on her back to get her moving. She kissed the baby and was a little surprised when Levi did the same.

"We'll get all this sorted out soon," Levi said. Maybe to Violet. Maybe to Alexa, too.

She prayed he was right. Alexa wanted Violet safe while they did the background checks on her next of kin and while they found whoever was behind the attacks.

Patty took the infant seat, and with Dallas and Chase on each side of her, they hurried toward the back exit. There was a black SUV parked right at the door, only about a yard away, and Alexa got one last glimpse of the baby's face before they got her inside. Within seconds Dallas drove away.

"Chase and Dallas will make sure they aren't followed," Levi said, watching until the SUV was out of sight.

Alexa didn't doubt that, and since it was daytime it would be easier to see if someone tried to go after them. Still, she doubted daylight would stop gunmen if they were determined to get to Violet. Of course, the upside to this was that if Marcos was behind the attacks, then Violet was now safe, because Marcos wasn't after the baby, only Alexa.

Levi maneuvered her back inside and shut the door. Jericho was right there waiting for them.

"You two should get out of here, too," Jericho insisted. He handed Levi some keys and a small piece of paper. "But don't go to the ranch."

Alexa was thankful for that. She didn't want a repeat of Scottie's visit, and by now it'd probably gotten around that Levi was protecting her.

"The keys are for Dexter's house," Jericho explained. "It's got a security system with motion detectors along the road. The sensors will go off if anyone drives up or tries to get near the house. Dexter had trouble with kids breaking in a while back, so that's why he had it installed. That's the security code, and park in the garage so no one knows you're there."

Alexa knew where the house was. About ten miles outside town. No nearby neighbors, and there was only one road leading to the property. It would be easy to spot an unexpected visitor. Easy to hear one, too, with the sensors.

"Please tell Dexter thank you," Alexa said.

Jericho nodded. "As soon as I can free up a deputy, I'll send him out to the house to help you keep watch."

It was a generous offer, but Alexa doubted the deputies would have much free time, especially since Jax would be out of that pool of possible deputies. No way would Jax want to be trapped under the same roof with her.

"I'll call you if I find out anything," Jericho added and opened the door. "Stay safe."

Levi thanked him, and he stepped outside to look around. He also took out his truck keys.

And his gun.

Even though his truck wasn't parked as close as the SUV had been, it was still only about fifteen yards away.

"Move fast," Levi instructed, and he used the remote on his key to unlock the truck doors.

Jericho walked out behind them, drawing his gun, as well, and Levi and she headed out into the parking lot. Not running exactly. But they didn't dawdle, either.

Alexa held her breath until they reached the truck. She threw open the door on the passenger's side at the same time Levi opened the driver's side door, and she started to get in.

She didn't get far.

Someone latched on to her feet, the jolt going through her entire body before she hit the ground.

Chapter Nine

Levi heard Alexa gasp, and he looked in her direction only to see her fall. Except it wasn't just a fall. It was as if someone had body slammed her.

With his gun still drawn, Levi scrambled across the seat, bracing himself for whatever he might see, but what he saw was some thug dragging a limp and lifeless Alexa behind one of the cruisers.

Damn. What was going on?

Levi didn't see any blood. Definitely hadn't heard a shot fired. He also hadn't seen anyone near the truck, so where had the guy been hiding? Maybe in the exact spot he'd just taken Alexa, that was where.

"Let go of her," Levi ordered, and he took aim at the man. Not that he could fire a shot. The goon had Alexa positioned in front of him like a human shield.

The man didn't answer, but he flashed Levi

a sick smile and started moving farther behind the cruiser and then to the other side, where Levi could no longer see them. Levi moved, too. Using the passenger's door for cover, he got out and tried to figure out what the heck he was up against.

"Jericho!" Levi shouted.

It was a big risk since the man could just gun him down, but Levi couldn't wait for backup. It was possible this man had a vehicle stashed nearby, and it was obvious that Alexa wasn't in any shape to fight back.

And Levi soon figured out why.

He spotted the stun gun on the ground.

That was why she'd been so lifeless. As bad as that was, and it was *bad*, it was still better than her being injured. However, unless he did something fast, an injury would be the least of their worries.

Levi heard the footsteps behind him and glanced over his shoulder to see Jericho coming out the back exit. He took up cover behind the edge of the building.

"There's at least one gunman by the cruiser," Levi called out to his brother. "He's got Alexa."

It felt like a punch to the gut just to say that aloud. He hadn't been careful enough. He hadn't protected her, and now Alexa might pay the ultimate price for his lapse.

Levi left the cover of the truck door and raced toward the back of the cruiser. He braced himself for shots to be fired. But no bullets. When he looked on the side of the cruiser, his heart dropped to his knees.

Alexa and the man weren't there.

The winter wind was gusting, making it hard for Levi to hear. It also didn't help that his heartbeat was slamming in his ears. Still, he picked through the noise and heard the footsteps.

They were coming from one cruiser over.

Levi dropped to the ground and looked underneath. Alexa was there by the rear tire, but it wasn't just one thug with her.

Now there were two.

There was a park just behind the sheriff's office, and it wouldn't have been hard for someone to hide back there and lie in wait. Still, this was a gutsy move, launching an attack like this in broad daylight.

Jericho ran from the building and dropped down next to Levi. He also had a look under the cruiser, and he cursed. Not just under his breath but out loud, as well.

"Really?" Jericho shouted. "You honestly think we'll just let you clowns leave with her?"

"You don't have much of a choice," one of them answered. "My advice? Back off and you won't get hurt."

No way would Levi just let them take her, but he heard something else he didn't want to hear. A car engine. And the sound wasn't coming from the parking lot but rather from the park. The goons no doubt had a getaway vehicle waiting for them there.

"Wouldn't shoot if I were you," the same goon called out. "Well, unless you want to make sure she gets killed real fast."

That told Levi exactly what he needed to know. Whoever was behind this wanted Alexa alive. If it was Marcos, maybe he wanted to torture her first. If it was Scottie's or Lockwood's hired guns, they could want information from her. That meant Levi had a chance to rescue her.

Not the safest chance. But nothing would be safe for her if these two managed to get her to a secondary location where heaven knew what would happen to her.

Levi went back to the ground again. And he took aim at the only semi-clear target he had. One of the men's legs.

He fired.

The howl of pain was instantaneous, letting Levi know that he'd hit his target.

"You bastard!" the man yelled, and he started to move. So did the other guy, who now had a hold of Alexa.

The shift in position gave Levi another opening because it left the wounded man in a vulnerable position. Levi fired a second shot into the guy's other leg. He wouldn't be running anywhere, but the clown did drop down, too, and he took aim.

At Levi.

Levi scrambled out of the way not a second too soon, and the shot blasted into his truck. He didn't wait for the guy to re-aim. Levi ran toward the front end of the cruiser, hoping that he could get the drop on the one who had Alexa.

Jericho scurried into the bed of the pickup, no doubt so he'd have a better vantage point and also because he could use it for cover. If his brother got a shot, Levi knew he would take it. There was no way Jericho would let this goon get Alexa into that waiting vehicle.

Levi stopped when he made it to the far edge of the front bumper, and he peered around the side. He caught just a glimpse of the man who had Alexa in a chokehold.

Before the shot came at him.

It ricocheted off the metal bumper.

The injured man might have two bullets in him, but it darn sure hadn't affected his aim. Levi needed to remedy that.

He leaned out again, and Levi kept his shot low so that it wouldn't hit Alexa. This time he double tapped the trigger, both bullets going into the wounded gunman's chest.

That stopped him.

And it clearly unnerved the second man, because he started to curse. "You must want her dead!"

Just the opposite. And while Levi wouldn't mind taking out both gunmen, it'd be better for the investigation if he had at least one of them alive.

Maybe not better for Alexa, though.

Her eyes were open. Wide with fear. Even though she couldn't move, she knew exactly what was happening to her. She also no doubt knew this could turn even deadlier than it already was.

"Put down your gun," Levi warned the man.

The guy's gaze was firing all around. Probably because he was trying to make sure Jericho wasn't sneaking up behind him. He also glanced in the direction of the sound of that car engine.

"There's at least fifteen yards between you and your getaway ride," Levi told him. "You're not going to make it, especially not dragging Alexa. Put down your gun, move away from her and let's talk."

"I can't talk to the cops," he said, but the guy was shaking now. Clearly in over his head.

Levi sweetened the pot a little. "We can give

you protection in exchange for the name of the person who hired you."

The man groaned, kicked his partner and then looked around again. Hopefully, he had reached the point where he'd figured out that he had zero chance of a clean escape. However, he was still armed, and Levi didn't want this to turn into a murder-suicide.

"You got me into this mess!" the man shouted, and he gave his partner another kick. The wounded man moaned in pain. Still alive. Barely. But he was bleeding out fast.

"If you want to help him and yourself, put down the gun," Levi bargained.

Levi saw it then. The surrender in the man's eyes. But it was only there for a split-second before he hurried against the cruiser and put the gun to Alexa's head.

No! This was not the way things were supposed to play out.

It took Levi a moment to realize why the guy had done that. There was the sound of footsteps. Someone running from the back of the parking lot toward them.

What the devil was *he* doing here?

ALEXA HADN'T THOUGHT her heart could pound any harder or faster. But she'd been wrong. For a few fleeting seconds she'd thought the goon holding her had been about to surrender.

Not now, though.

Now he had his gun jammed against her temple, and as unsteady as he was, he might just pull the trigger.

Alexa tried to move, something she'd been attempting since this insane attack had first happened. No luck. The stun gun had done its job, and she couldn't make her arms or legs work. She couldn't even call out to Levi to tell him to stay down.

He wouldn't listen to her anyway, of course.

But she wanted to try. She didn't want him or his brother hurt trying to protect her.

"You idiot!" Levi snarled, and it took her a moment to realize he wasn't talking to the gunman, but rather to someone who had ducked behind the cruiser next to the gunman and her.

Lockwood.

"I can help," Lockwood shouted back.

She certainly hadn't expected him to show up here.

Alexa doubted Lockwood would have come this close if these were his own hired guns. Well, he might if he wanted to look innocent. What better way to do that than to pretend he was trying to put an end to this kidnapping attempt? Especially since the attempt had been botched.

One man was dying and there was no clean escape for the other.

"There's no one in the getaway car," Lockwood added. "It's just these two jokers, and they left the engine running."

Alexa wasn't sure she believed the marshal, and she seriously doubted that Levi would just trust him. But if Lockwood was telling the truth, it meant this thug didn't have anyone else to help him. That was far better than the alternative, but it didn't help her much now. After all, it would only take one person to kill her, Levi and Jericho, and the gunman was using her to prevent the lawmen from having a clean shot.

She needed to do something to remedy that.

Alexa concentrated on flexing the muscles in her arm. She managed to wiggle her fingers a little. Not much, but it was a start, and with each passing second it meant she would get more and more feeling back.

More and more fear, too.

Choking back those fears, she said another prayer for the protection detail that had whisked Violet away. Maybe there wasn't a second team of hired guns going after them. That was all the more reason to end this now so she could check on them.

"Back off!" the gunman yelled. "All of you. So help me, I'll kill her."

He would. Alexa could feel the desperation in him. But her will to live was even stronger than that. She forced herself to concentrate on moving her right arm, since it was next to her captor's stomach. She doubted she could do much, but she prayed it would be enough.

The wounded man groaned again, and his breath rattled in his throat. His last breath. Something the man holding her must have understood, because he looked down at his fallen partner. It wasn't much of a distraction, but it might be the only one she could get.

Alexa jammed her elbow into the man and she tumbled forward, hoping to get out of his grip. She wasn't even sure she'd succeeded when she heard the blast.

Oh, God.

Had she been shot?

Everything seemed to move fast but in slow motion, too. She didn't feel any pain. Didn't feel much of anything, even when she hit the concrete. However, she didn't hit it alone.

Her captor dropped down right beside her.

Their eyes met, but his were blank. Lifeless. And that was when Alexa saw the wound to his head. Someone had shot him.

She heard the footsteps hurrying toward her, and while Alexa still couldn't move that well, she tried to get up. Thankfully, Levi helped her with that. He scooped her up in his arms and ran back into the sheriff's office. Jericho and Lockwood were right behind them, but Jericho kept the door open, looking out. He kept his gun ready, too, probably because despite what Lockwood had said, there could be other hired thugs out there.

Levi took her to the side of the break room and he eased her onto a cot. He pushed her hair from her face, no doubt checking for injuries, and she was relieved when she saw the relief in his own eyes.

Relief, however, that Levi didn't extend to Lockwood.

"You killed him," Levi said to Lockwood.

Lockwood nodded. "I had the shot and I took it. I saved Alexa."

So, Lockwood had been the one who'd taken out the gunman. Alexa managed to tell him thanks, but she still wasn't so sure that Lockwood had done this for her. Obviously, Levi wasn't positive, either, because he volleyed glances between the marshal and her.

"The ambulance is on the way," Mack called out to them. "How many will the medics be picking up?"

"The gunmen are both dead," Levi answered. "But Alexa needs to go to the hospital."

She shook her head. "Check on the baby."

The words weren't exactly clear, but Levi understood them because he took out his phone and fired off a text. It only took a few seconds for him to get a response from Chase, and Levi held it up for her to see.

Everything's fine here.

Thank God. That was exactly what she needed to know, but Alexa had no idea if things were fine right here in the sheriff's office. They could be in the room with the person trying to kill her.

Except this hadn't been a murder attempt.

Those men had definitely been trying to kidnap her. And the question she had was why? However, she doubted she'd get the answer from Lockwood. If he was innocent, he wouldn't know why those men had come after her, and if he was guilty, he wouldn't just tell them the truth.

Levi checked her again, his hand lingering on her cheek for several seconds, before he stood and faced Lockwood. "Why were you in the parking lot?"

Lockwood pulled back his shoulders. Obviously not pleased with Levi's tone. But Alexa was pleased. She had the same question, and tone, for Lockwood because it seemed a strange coincidence that he would arrive at the time of the attack.

"I came to talk to the sheriff," Lockwood said, but he didn't look at Jericho. He kept his narrowed gaze on Levi.

"So, talk," Jericho snapped, still keeping watch.

Lockwood's eyes narrowed even more. "The cops over in Junction Ridge found a body this morning," he said. Now his attention went to Alexa. "It's a woman, and they're pretty sure it could be Tasha."

Chapter Ten

Levi listened to what Jericho was telling him. It was an important update on Scottie, but his attention was on Alexa. Exactly where it'd been since they'd arrived at Dexter's house and where his attention would likely stay until he was certain she was indeed as all right as she claimed.

He wasn't convinced.

At least she was moving again. Well, sort of. Once they'd gotten into the house, locked up and set the security alarm, Alexa had dropped down on to the sofa. Clearly shaken. And also clearly waiting for news not just on the woman's body that'd been found, but she undoubtedly wanted to hear from Marshal Walker so they'd know he'd made it to the safe house with the baby.

Levi could help her with the last part but not the first.

"I'll tell Alexa," Levi assured his brother, and he ended the call.

"Is Violet safe?" Alexa asked right off.

Levi nodded. "Marshal Walker called Jericho and told him no one followed them to the safe house, and Violet is all settled in."

Alexa nodded, too. "Good. I'm glad she's okay. I'm not sure I could have dealt with it if she hadn't been."

Probably not. Of course, she wasn't exactly dealing with everything else, either. Her nerves were raw and right at the surface. Any bit of bad news now could break her, and that was why Levi continued with the last of the good news he did have. Maybe it would help take some of that worry and fear out of her eyes.

"Marshal Walker talked with his boss," Levi continued. "And you don't have to go back into the marshals' custody. Especially not Lockwood's. As long as you stay in protective custody, that'll work for them."

"Thank you. And I'll thank Marshal Walker, too," she said.

But Levi wasn't sure she should be thankful that she was staying with him. After all, he'd done a really bad job of keeping her safe so far. Two attacks in two days, and that wasn't counting the one that had sent her running to him in the first place. Whoever was behind this was damn persistent, and Levi doubted the snake would just give up because two more of his hired guns had been killed.

After hearing the two pieces of good news, Alexa did look relieved, but the look didn't last long. Her forehead bunched up again. "Is there anything about the body?"

"No ID yet, but it shouldn't be much longer." Actually, it could come at any time now.

"I could ID her if they send me a picture," she offered. It was probably the last thing she wanted to see if it was indeed Tasha, but other than asking Scottie, Alexa was their best bet at making a facial ID.

But there was a problem.

One that Levi wouldn't mention to her just yet. The dead woman's face had been, well, damaged. In part, by the gunshot wounds to her head. Also in part because the killer had tossed her body into a ravine, and the fall had done even more damage. There were broken bones and postmortem injuries.

"You said the gunman only shot Tasha once?" he asked.

"Yes." She stared at him. "Why?"

"Because this woman had three gunshot wounds to the back and head."

More relief. Again, short-lived. Because Alexa must have realized that the killer could have shot

Tasha two more times after Alexa had fled with the baby.

"The cops are working on getting Tasha's dental records," Levi added. "If they match the body, then you won't have to try to make the ID."

Levi was really hoping that would happen while still holding out hope the body wasn't Tasha's. The cops in Junction Ridge hadn't been able to give them much of a physical description of the DB, only that it was a woman about five foot five and with brown hair. Since there was another missing woman, a known drug dealer, who also matched the description, there was still a chance. Added to that, Junction Ridge was a good hundred miles from the gas station where Tasha and Alexa had been attacked.

"She could still be alive," Levi reminded her, going with the theory that Tasha had faked her own death to escape Scottie. If it was true, then it would mean Violet wasn't an orphan.

And that the baby would eventually have some place to go.

Which brought him to the second part of the conversation he'd just had with Jericho.

"Brett Mendoza has two aunts, both in their early fifties, and Child Services will ask them if they're willing to take the baby," he explained.

"Are they fit to raise Violet?" she asked.

"No indications that they aren't, but they'll

be checked out. That could take a while. Child Services has agreed to back off as long as Violet's under the marshals' protection, but eventually she'll be placed with either the aunts or someone else, so it'll be a permanent custody arrangement for her."

"I want her," Alexa jumped to say. But again, the doubt crept into her eyes.

Levi knew why.

He sank down on the sofa next to her. Not just because she looked as if she needed some close contact, but also because it put him in a better position to look out the window. There'd been no sign that anyone had followed them. No sign of other gunmen. Nor had anything or anyone tripped the sensors along the road. But Levi wouldn't take any more chances with her life.

"Even if the aunts turn out to be unfit, I can't take Violet as long as Marcos is after me," Alexa added. "And even after the trial, he might still be after me."

Levi sure couldn't argue with that. Marcos could still control his henchmen from behind bars. Which meant unless something drastic happened, Alexa would have to go back into WITSEC. A new identity, a new life. One where she'd always be looking over her shoulder for a would-be killer.

Hardly a good life for a baby.

"If it doesn't work out with the aunts, there are plenty of good families out there who'd love to adopt her," Levi said. Then, he frowned.

Heck.

There it was again. That tugging feeling in his heart. He didn't want to see Violet handed off to strangers. He'd diapered her, fed her and walked the floor with her when she wouldn't hush crying. That'd obviously created some kind of bond that couldn't happen since he wasn't exactly stellar father material.

"Something else has you worried." Alexa touched his face, right between his eyebrows. "What is it?"

It really wasn't something he could keep from her, and it was news they'd expected. "Scottie's already out of jail."

Alexa took a deep, weary breath. "Is there any way we can find out who he phoned from the sheriff's office? Because he could have ordered the attack with that call."

Levi agreed. "We're getting a court order for his phone records." Though he hated to tell Alexa that if Scottie had indeed triggered that attack, then he'd probably used a prepaid cell or some other phone that couldn't be traced back to those hired guns.

Of course, even if Scottie had actually made the call to his attorney and not a pair of gunmen, that didn't mean he hadn't given the order to his lawyer to put the attack into motion. Still, a court order might unnerve Scottie a little.

"Chase is doing okay?" she asked.

Levi hadn't expected the question. Not because his brother hadn't been on his mind. But with everything else going on, he was surprised Alexa had remembered that only a few weeks ago Chase had been knifed by the Moonlight Strangler.

"He's recovering," Levi settled for saying. Like him, though, Chase had this need to catch the killer. "When Violet no longer needs protective custody, then Chase will almost certainly go on the hunt again for the Moonlight Strangler."

She lifted her eyes, met his gaze. "And Jax and you will join him."

No sense denying the obvious, so Levi just nodded. "You will, too?"

Alexa nodded, as well. "As best I can. If I'm in WITSEC that limits how much I can do without drawing attention to myself. Then again, I might not have to look for long. After all, the Moonlight Strangler found me once, and he can find me again."

Definitely not a comfortable thought. It didn't matter that the killer had said he would leave her alone, because there was no way she would trust him. No way would she get a decent night's sleep until he was either behind bars or in the grave.

Levi checked out the window again, and this time Alexa noticed. She turned, her attention landing on the road where Levi kept glancing.

No one was there.

"You're expecting the worst," she said.

"I just want to be ready if something goes wrong again," he corrected. "I nearly got you killed today."

She huffed. But it wasn't exactly a huff from anger because tears watered her eyes. "No. I nearly got you killed. And your brother. Heck, everyone in the sheriff's office."

The tears didn't stay in her eyes. They spilled down her cheeks, and Levi did something he was certain he would regret. He pulled Alexa into his arms. Despite the cruddy situation and those tears, he felt the very thing he didn't want to feel.

The heat.

Oh, yes. It was there mixed with all the fresh emotions and spent adrenaline from the latest attack.

"You don't want this," Alexa whispered.

Even though she didn't qualify what she meant by *this*, Levi made a sound of agreement. He didn't want the problems that could come from the attraction he was feeling for her.

But he did want her.

And he did something about it when she leaned back to look at him. He slipped his hand around the back of her neck and kissed her.

No tug this time. It felt like a truck had hit him in the chest. Oh, man. He hadn't wanted her to taste like something he was certain he could never get enough of. He'd wanted the kiss to satisfy this need stirring inside him.

Didn't happen.

The need soared.

Alexa did her part to make that happen. She certainly didn't move away or stop him. She kissed him right back, along with making a silky little sound of pleasure that Levi was sure could be his undoing.

For a moment he thought the buzzing sound he was hearing was from the buzz he was getting from the kiss. But it was his phone. He snapped back from her so he could take it out of his pocket, and he saw Jericho's name on the screen.

Probably not good news.

That was why Levi started to get up and move away from Alexa. That and he needed a second to cool down his body, something that wouldn't happen if he stayed so close to her. But she took hold of his arm.

"Please, put the call on speaker. I need to hear what Jericho has to say," she insisted.

Well, she certainly had a right to hear it since it would likely involve her in some way, but Levi had hoped to be able to buffer the news. But she was right. She would need to hear this. And deal with it.

"Just got a call from Junction Ridge," Jericho greeted the moment Levi answered. He glanced through some notes he'd taken. "The dead body is Tasha."

Alexa's breath trembled. So did she, and Levi sank back down beside her.

"They're sure?" Levi asked, already knowing that the answer would be yes.

"They got a confirmation from dental records. We'll run the DNA to double-check. We can get Tasha's DNA from that amnio test that you mentioned she had a while back and compare it to the body." Jericho glanced at the notes again. "The cause of death was the gunshot wound to the back of the head."

Just as Alexa had said.

"All the other wounds, including the two additional gunshots, happened after her death," Jericho explained.

"Overkill," Alexa whispered.

Yeah, it was, which would point to Scottie. But that seemed almost too convenient unless Scottie was going for some kind of reverse psychology.

But Levi wasn't ready to take Lockwood or Marcos off that list.

Lockwood could have hired those goons to go after Alexa, and they could have killed Tasha by mistake.

"I'll have to let Child Services know," Jericho added. "But that doesn't need to happen today. It's not as if I don't have plenty to keep me busy."

True, and Levi wished it was safe enough for him to be there with Alexa. "Anything yet on the two dead gunmen?"

"No. The ME's finishing up, and I'm about to head out to examine the scene." Jericho paused. "Lockwood's still here, too."

"Why?" Alexa immediately asked.

"To hell if I know. I haven't exactly put out the welcome mat for him. He's making calls and doing a lot of pacing. When I get off the phone I'm giving him the boot. He can find another place to hang out until I'm dead sure he's not trying to kill us."

"Good idea. Email me whatever reports I can do here," Levi said. "I'll use Dexter's computer."

"Just do your statement and take Alexa's when you can. Everything okay there?" Jericho asked.

Levi purposely didn't look at her. Or her mouth. "Fine." It wasn't anywhere close to the truth, and Jericho likely knew that. "We can talk more after you've had a chance to examine those dead gunmen," Levi added, and he ended the call.

Silence followed.

He could hear Alexa's breathing. It was too fast, and the blasted tears were within seconds of starting again. She had a reason to cry. A reason to fall into a thousand little pieces, and Levi wasn't sure how to stop it.

So, he kissed her.

It barely qualified as a kiss. More of a peck of reassurance, the kind that people who'd been in a relationship for a long time gave each other. In other words, definitely not their kind of kiss.

Alexa looked at him, and he couldn't be certain but she seemed thankful he'd delivered that peck. Thankfully, he'd stopped the tears. At least, that was how the look started out.

Then it changed.

Big time.

Levi wasn't sure which of them made the first move. They seemed to come together at once. Her, putting her arms around his neck. Him, dragging her to him. He kissed her again. Same taste.

But different from that other real kiss.

Everything was different.

After nearly dying, this didn't seem like such a big mistake, but it was. Knowing that, however, didn't stop him. Levi snapped her closer until she was plastered right against him, and he deepened the kiss.

This need for her wasn't what he wanted. Far from it. He wanted to feel the calm detachment that would have made his life so much easier. Didn't happen. No detachment. Instead, the kiss turned to fire, a fire so hot that kisses were only going to fuel it even more.

He dropped some of those kisses on her neck. And went even lower. Until that wasn't enough, either, and Levi shoved up her top. She helped, not that it was actually helping, but Alexa opened the front hook of her bra, and her breasts spilled out into his hands.

That was a game changer.

Of course, he lowered his head and kissed her breasts. Despite the urgency building between them, he took his time. When he was done, when Alexa's breath was ragged and her hands working hard to touch him, he circled her nipples with his fingers and went after her mouth again.

She didn't just slide right into the kiss, though. Alexa fought first with his shoulder holster. When she couldn't get that off him, she went after the buttons on his shirt. And she hit pay dirt when her mouth landed on his chest.

Oh, man.

So not the direction he should be going.

Knowing that didn't stop him or slow him down. Levi went after the zipper on her jeans. She helped without breaking those maddening kisses she had now taken to his stomach.

"Take off your jeans," he insisted.

This would have been a really good time for her to say they needed to stop. She didn't. "You take them off."

Because he was obviously stupid right now, that was exactly what he did. Not just her jeans, either. Levi pulled off her panties with them.

"Don't change your mind," she said.

It was advice Levi knew he shouldn't take. But he just kept moving this forward. Just kept escalating it. And he didn't exactly do it with a lot of finesse, either.

He should pick Alexa up and take her to the guest room, but his body was urging him on and he didn't want to waste the couple of minutes it'd take him to do that. Instead, they maneuvered around on the sofa while Alexa unzipped him and freed him from his boxers.

Levi didn't change his mind. He pushed into her, the pleasure slamming into him. He had to take a second to catch his breath. And nearly lost it again when he saw her face.

She was beautiful, and it wasn't the sex talking. Alexa was a knockout, and she was looking up at him as if giving him permission to explore every inch of her with every inch of him. Levi started to do just that.

And then he stopped.

"No condom," he somehow managed to get out.

Alexa shook her head as if it didn't matter, but then her eyes widened. "I'm not on the pill."

"Hell." And because he couldn't think of anything else to say, he repeated the one word a couple of times.

Making the mistake of having sex with someone he was protecting was one thing, but getting her pregnant would take this to new realms of stupidity. Thankfully, it was enough to get him to move off her.

Way off.

Levi dropped to a sitting position on the floor, because he figured it would only add to the stupidity if he was still touching her.

"I'm sorry." Alexa sat up, too, and immediately started grappling to get back on her clothes.

Good.

Because seeing her naked wasn't going to help this, either. Levi fixed his jeans. Not easy to do with his erection demanding that he finish what they'd started. The demand was so strong that

Levi considered running to Dexter's medicine cabinet to see if he had any condoms.

Talk about fanning a flame that shouldn't be fanned.

But Levi didn't have to resist that particular temptation, because his phone buzzed. It was Jericho again, which meant it had to be important. Levi answered it, and hoped his brother wouldn't pick up on the weird vibes there were now in the room.

"We might have found something," Jericho said. "I've got to process the evidence and that'll take a while, but if it tells me what I think it's going to tell me, we should be able to make an arrest."

Levi had plenty of questions but went with the obvious one. "Who?"

"Marcos. We finally might have something to put him in a cell for the rest of his scummy life."

Chapter Eleven

Alexa wasn't sure she could sit still much longer and wait for Marcos to arrive. Everything inside her was twisting and churning, and she had nowhere to aim all that nervous energy.

Unlike Levi.

Since they'd arrived at the sheriff's office, he'd been at his desk working. Either talking to someone on the phone or writing up reports about the attack in the parking lot. Actually, that was what he'd been doing since the day before when Jericho had first called about the possible evidence he'd found against Marcos. Levi certainly hadn't jumped into a conversation with her about what'd happened on the sofa.

And Alexa wasn't sure if she should be thankful for that or not.

It'd been a mistake, even if it hadn't actually felt like one. They had so many more things that should have their attention, and their lives were still on the line. The last thing they should be doing was having sex. Or rather attempting sex.

No way should that happen.

Alexa repeated that reminder to herself and forced her attention off Levi. That didn't last long at all. Her gaze went right back to him.

Of course, she'd always known he was attractive. Hard not to see that then and now since she was seated only two desks away from him. Levi had definitely inherited those hot Crockett genes. But he'd also been hands off because of the bad blood between his family and her. That bad blood, though, hadn't been enough to stop the attraction from boiling over, and now Levi was clearly trying to put as much emotional distance between them as possible.

And it was working.

Well, it had been until he lifted his head and their eyes met. He only held the connection for a few seconds. More than enough for her to feel the heat again. More than enough for him, too, since he glanced away, but not before looking thoroughly disgusted with himself.

Alexa was so focused on him that she got a little jolt when someone plopped a disposable cup of coffee with her name written on it in front of her.

Jax.

Like Jericho and Mack, Jax had been at the

sheriff's office when Levi and she had arrived. It made sense, after all, because he was a deputy, but Alexa didn't think it was her imagination that his family had made sure Jax didn't have to spend too much time around her. However, Jax hadn't avoided her.

Now she was the one who did some gaze dodging. It was hard for her to look Jax in the eyes and not be reminded of what'd happened to Paige.

"It's decaf," Jax said, tipping his head to the cup. "I had it delivered from the diner. We only have the rocket-fuel coffee here in the office, and you didn't look as if you needed any more caffeine. Levi said you take it black, so that's how I ordered it."

No way could she dodge his gaze after that. "Thanks. I am pretty wired up already."

He made a sound to indicate he understood. And he no doubt did. Marcos would be there any minute. Of course, she could hide in Jericho's office—something both Jericho and Levi were insisting she do—but Alexa wanted to hear what Marcos had to say about what'd been found in the hired gunmen's vehicle.

Some cash with Marcos's prints on it.

And one of the gunmen had scrawled Marcos's private phone number on his hand. It was enough evidence for SAPD to pick up Marcos and escort him to Appaloosa Pass for an interrogation, but it might not be enough to convict him.

"Marcos will find a way out of this." Alexa hadn't actually meant to say that aloud, but Jax made another of those sounds to let her know he understood. And agreed with her.

"He'll say it's a setup." Jax had a sip of his own coffee. "It certainly smacks of one. He's not stupid."

"No, but maybe the hired guns were. Maybe they weren't supposed to write down that number, bring the money. Or get killed so we could find those things."

"So, either a setup or dumb killers." Jax shrugged. "Either way, we get another shot at interrogating Marcos. Levi's going to have a go at him this time. Maybe Marcos will lose his temper and admit to everything. That way we can lock him up and you'll be safer than you were when you woke up this morning."

Jax's tone was actually hopeful. Something Alexa wasn't feeling. And he wasn't scowling at her. She hated to spoil the moment, if it was indeed a moment, but she was confused as to why he wasn't avoiding her. Or scowling at her.

"I'm sorry about your friend, Tasha, being killed," Jax continued. "Sorry about the baby, too."

Violet. She was never far from Alexa's mind.

Never far from her fears, either. She'd already called Marshal Walker twice this morning. All was well at the safe house, but Alexa couldn't help but worry that the worst could, and would, happen.

"Jericho said there weren't any family members who'd stepped up yet to take custody of the baby," Jax added.

"No. We're waiting to hear back from two aunts."

"But you want her." Not a question exactly. Nor was there any condemnation in Jax's voice.

"Why are you being nice to me?" she asked.

Jax glanced at Levi. "Because of him. Want to talk about what's going on between my brother and you?"

"No."

The corner of Jax's mouth lifted. "That's what Levi said, too."

"You actually asked him?"

"Tried to ask him," Jax corrected. He leaned in, lowered his voice. "Levi seems to think I need to be protected from you. I don't."

Levi obviously hadn't missed Jax's and her conversation because he ended his call and made a beeline toward them. "Is everything okay?"

"Sure," Jax answered before Alexa could say anything. "Enjoy your decaf," he added and then strolled away.

Levi stood there volleying glances between her and his brother, and while he wasn't glaring, it was obvious he wanted to know what Jax and she had been discussing. It was also obvious he didn't want Jax upset.

"Jax and I were just talking about Tasha and the baby. Oh, he brought me coffee, of course." She touched the outside of the cup just above the cardboard sleeve. Still too hot to drink. "I didn't say anything about Paige. Or anything else."

"*Anything else?*" Levi repeated. "Is that code for what happened between us?"

Alexa debated her answer and went with the truth. "Yes. He said he'd asked you about it, but you didn't volunteer anything. Neither did I." She paused. "Mainly because I had no idea what to volunteer."

And there it was, the opening for him to discuss this.

Or not.

Levi waited so long to answer that she thought he might just turn away and get back to work. He didn't. "You complicate things for me," he said finally.

She nearly smiled. Nearly. "And you complicate things for me. I have no prospects of a future. A safe, normal future anyway, and the last thing I need is a lover that I want."

Now it seemed as if he nearly smiled, but it

wasn't from humor. No, she recognized frustration when she saw it. "I guess you're saying we could never be friends with benefits."

No, casual sex was out. Not her style. Nor Levi's, though she was sure that with his looks he'd had plenty of opportunities in that particular area.

"Are we friends?" she asked.

"Allies," he corrected. Then frowned. "Friends." After that admission he cursed, his voice a little too loud, because it drew the attention of both his brothers.

Levi waved them off and he looked at her. Not just an ordinary look. One that could have melted chrome. "And if there'd been a condom nearby, we'd be having a different conversation because we would have already had sex."

Oh, this was so not a good time to feel that heat trickle through her. Not a good time to remember his kiss. His touch.

And the rest of him.

But Alexa remembered and was afraid that she always would. Great day. She was really racing toward that broken heart, and there didn't seem to be anything she could do to stop it.

Again, Alexa got so caught up in her thoughts, and Levi, that the sound of someone saying her name gave her a jolt. But it was only Jericho making his way toward them.

"Did Marcos weasel out of coming here?" she asked.

Jericho shook his head. "This is about that chat room, the one the Moonlight Strangler told you to use."

Alexa hadn't forgotten about it, but she'd figured it was a long shot. "And?"

"The FBI set up a profile for you and made some posts, and we got a response." Jericho handed her a sheet of paper.

Alexa couldn't take it fast enough. Like the other message, it was short.

She read it aloud. "'Alexa-girl, good to hear from you. Well, if it's really you. We both know how these things work, and I'll watch my p's and q's so your Fed friends don't use this.'"

Of course, he would be cautious. If this was indeed the killer and not some groupie playing games. But then, she was almost certain the letter was real, so maybe this was, too.

"'A warning,'" she continued to read. "'You've got a problem child on your hands. Watch out for him and tell him I don't like him stealing my letters. Sleep well, Alexa-girl.'"

"Scottie," Levi said. "If the Moonlight Strangler saw him steal the letter, that means he probably had your place under surveillance."

Yes and it also meant he might be watching her now. That would only add to her nightmares.

"The FBI will let us know if there are any other messages," Jericho told her. He took the paper and headed back to the desk to make yet another call.

"You okay?" Levi asked her.

Not really. And she got another jolt when she looked up and saw Marcos. Not alone. He was being escorted by two uniformed cops from the SAPD and a man wearing a suit. His new lawyer, probably.

"Good morning, Alexa," Marcos said, his attention going straight to her. "Here to falsely accuse me of something else?"

Alexa stood. "No. I'm here to see how you'll try to squirm your way out of this." Thank goodness she sounded strong, but she was still shaking from that attack and the message from the Moonlight Strangler. Seeing the man who might be responsible certainly didn't help.

What did help was that Levi went to her side, silently supporting her. Marcos noticed. Smiled. As if he knew exactly what was going on between them. He didn't, because even Alexa didn't know that.

"This way," Levi told Marcos and his entourage, and he pointed to the interrogation room.

"No need to sit down," Marcos insisted. "I think I can clear this all up in a matter of a few seconds. I'm innocent. I didn't hire those two men or anyone else to come after you."

"Oh, yeah?" Levi asked, and he didn't bother to take out the sarcasm. "And you think we'll just take your word for it?"

"No, but I don't think you're so biased that you won't listen to the facts. My wallet was stolen yesterday, and I'm sure the money you found with my prints was taken from my stolen wallet."

"Convenient," Levi remarked.

"The truth. I filed a police report." Marcos snapped his fingers at the lawyer, and the man handed Levi some papers. It was indeed a police report, and it'd been filed hours before the attack.

Sweet heaven. This could allow Marcos to walk, but there was the other evidence against him.

"How'd your phone number get on the gunman's hand?" she asked.

Marcos shrugged. "That number is private, but plenty of people have it. Including you since you did some work for me."

Alexa had to nod. It was true. She had indeed done some PI work for him, and that was how she'd discovered his illegal activities.

Marcos didn't even acknowledge her nod. He

looked at Levi instead. "Come on—can't you see someone's trying to set me up?"

Levi's hands went to his hips. "And who would do that to you?"

Marcos didn't jump to answer. He first exchanged a short whispered conversation with his attorney before he turned and faced Levi again. "I think it's the person who's really behind that whole money laundering and extortion operation. He set me up then to take the fall by leaving so-called evidence for Alexa to find, and now he's trying to set me up again."

"Does this person have a name?" Levi snapped.

"Yes." A muscle flickered in Marcos's jaw. "It's Marshal Lockwood."

LEVI JUST STARED at Marcos, waiting for the man to add more to that accusation. But he didn't. Instead, he had another whispered conversation with his lawyer. However, his lawyer didn't appear to be pleased about what his client had just said.

Welcome to the club.

Levi didn't mind Marcos accusing Lockwood of anything. Plain and simple, he had his own concerns about the marshal. But Levi seriously doubted Marcos's blabbering was anything more than just that.

Blabbering.

"The last time we questioned you here in the sheriff's office, you said Lockwood didn't have anything to do with your criminal operation," Levi reminded him.

"It's not my operation. It's Lockwood's. He's the one who put it together and then set me up to take the fall for him."

Alexa shook her head. "When I worked for you, I didn't see anything related to Lockwood."

"Because he didn't use his real name, of course."

She huffed and looked about as skeptical as Levi felt. "And why are you just now bringing this up?" Levi asked.

"Because my lawyers have advised me not to get into too many details since this will be part of my defense at the trial, but I'm sick and tired of being accused of trying to kill you." Marcos jabbed his index finger at Alexa. "If I wanted you dead, you already would be."

His lawyer took hold of him, but Marcos shook off his grip. "Just think it through, Alexa. There were other names involved in that operation. One of those names is the alias Lockwood used. Why don't you get your cowboy cop here to find out which one?"

Levi had studied the case against Marcos. There were other names, but neither the FBI nor

SAPD had been able to figure out the real identities. Was it possible Lockwood was one of them and that Marcos was telling the truth? Of course, Marcos had a reason to lie. He'd been charged because of that criminal operation. Lockwood hadn't been.

"This way." Levi pointed to the interrogation room again. "Let's put all this down on paper and make it official."

The lawyer clearly didn't like that, but Marcos didn't put up even a token objection. He followed Levi down the hall, his lawyer trailing behind him.

"We've got some paperwork we need to drop off at the DA's office," one of the SAPD cops said. "Unless you need us here, we'll be back in about a half hour."

"Take your time," Levi offered. He doubted this was going to be a speedy interrogation.

"I've been telling you all along that I'm not guilty," Marcos insisted.

Levi ignored him for the time being and looked back to check on Alexa. To see how she was handling all this. Not well. But then, it'd been a very emotional past couple days for her. The muscles in her face and shoulders were stiff, and she had such a grip on the coffee cup that he was surprised she hadn't crushed it.

"I'll be a few seconds," Levi said to Marcos

and the lawyer, and he shut the door of the interrogation room, staying in the hall with her.

Jericho must have realized he needed a moment because his brother stepped into the observation room where he'd no doubt be watching when Levi questioned Marcos. Alexa would, too, and that wouldn't help her nerves any.

"I could have screwed up," she said, her voice trembling a little. "I could have seen Lockwood's alias on those records and not realized he was the actual head of the operation."

"That's possible," Levi acknowledged. "Though it's not really a screw-up. Unless you have ESP, there's no way you could have known any of those names belonged to Lockwood. And maybe one of the names does. Marcos's bail will be revoked if any of these new charges stick, and this might be his way of making sure that doesn't happen."

She looked up at him. Nodded. Of course, considering everything it would be better if Lockwood was the mastermind, because then it could mean Marcos was telling the truth about wanting her dead.

However, Levi wasn't about to trust Marcos, and he was sure Alexa wasn't about to, either.

"I need to talk to James Moser again," she said. "He was the one who initially clued me in to the possibility of Lockwood's guilt, and he might know more."

Levi really had wanted to wait to tell her this news, but it was obvious that Alexa would be trying to call James soon. Maybe while he was interrogating Marcos. "James is missing."

Alexa sucked in her breath. "What?"

"I figured you had enough to deal with, so I decided to hold off telling you. SAPD's still looking for him."

"Oh, God. Something bad could have happened to him."

Yeah, it could have, but that wasn't what he said to Alexa. "Don't borrow trouble. James is a smart PI, and he might be just lying low because he knows someone could be after him." He hoped that was true anyway. "I'll call for an update about James when I'm finished with Marcos."

And because he thought they both could use it, he brushed a kiss on her cheek. A chaste one considering how close they'd come to having sex. "Just go in the observation room with Jericho and wait for me."

Levi opened the door for her to do just that, but Alexa hadn't even taken a step inside when the front door flew open and a man barreled in.

Scottie.

Levi automatically drew his gun and stepped in front of her.

Scottie wasn't armed, though, and he wasn't

wearing his usual bulky coat. In fact, he looked disheveled and was gulping in large breaths.

"Don't!" Scottie shouted, pointed to Alexa.

Levi wasn't sure if that was some kind of threat, but he didn't want to take any chances. He also didn't have time to deal with this clown when he already had another one waiting for him.

Scottie ran toward them, staggering a few steps. "Don't drink that."

And it took Levi a moment to realize Scottie was pointing at the cup Alexa was holding.

"What's this about?" Levi asked the man.

"That." Scottie pointed to the cup again. "Someone's trying to kill Alexa. The coffee's been poisoned."

Chapter Twelve

Before Scottie's words even sank in, Levi had snatched the cup from her hand. "Are you all right?" Levi asked her, the concern all over his face.

Alexa managed to nod. "I didn't drink any. It was too hot."

All the others came rushing toward her. Jericho, Mack and even Jax. Jax was shaking his head before he even reached her.

"I didn't put anything in it," he said as if she needed to hear it. She didn't. Jax might not be her friend, but he was a cop. A good one. And he wouldn't try to poison her.

In fact, maybe no one had tried to do that. After all, the accusation had come from a man she didn't trust: Scottie.

"I know you didn't," she assured Jax and then turned to Scottie. "What makes you think it was poisoned?" Alexa demanded.

Levi's glare let Scottie know that he was demanding the same information.

Scottie pointed to the diner across the street. "I overheard a waitress and a busboy talking. She asked him if he'd put the *stuff* in the right cup, and he said he had because it had Alexa's name on it. Then, she asked if it'd kill Alexa, and the busboy said he didn't know, that his job was just to doctor the coffee."

Heavens. Was it true? Had someone just tried to kill her again? Even though Alexa hadn't taken even a sip of the coffee, she felt her stomach tighten into a hard, painful knot.

"Which waitress and busboy?" Jericho asked.

Scottie touched his fingers to his head and looked shaken. Or rather pretending to look that way. "She has short brown hair. Young, maybe twenty. The busboy was probably about the same age. Black hair."

Levi glanced at Jericho. "Does that sound like anyone you know?"

"No," Jericho answered. He took the cup from Levi and handed it to Mack. "Have the lab pick this up to be analyzed ASAP. I'm going across the street to have a chat with this waitress and busboy." He headed for the door but not before giving Scottie a sharp look. "And so help me God, this had better not be some kind of sick game you're playing."

Or a ruse to get to her again.

Levi must have had the same thought because he moved her into the doorway of the observation room and he stayed in the hall, guarding her once again. Jax drew his gun and went to the front door, no doubt so he could provide backup to Jericho if his brother needed it. His new position also put him closer to Scottie, and Jax volleyed his attention between Scottie and the diner.

"Is it possible the waitress and busboy are new, that they could have been planted in the diner?" she asked.

Levi nodded. "Jericho will sort it all out, though."

Yes, but she hoped that sorting out didn't launch another attack. If the waitress and busboy had indeed tried to kill her, then they might also try to kill Jericho so they could escape. If they hadn't already gotten out of the diner.

Alexa glanced through the observation mirror and spotted Marcos. She expected to see him smiling. He wasn't. He was having another whispered conversation with his lawyer, and both men were looking worried. Maybe because Marcos thought he might be blamed for this.

"You stay here," she heard Mack say to Scottie, and the deputy made his way back toward them. "I've bagged the coffee and a CSI is on the way over here to pick it up to take it to the lab. It'll be a while before we know anything."

Levi stared at Scottie. "But I can find out some things from you right now. Why are you here in town?"

The question seemed to throw Scottie for a moment. Maybe because his attention was focused on the diner. Not that he could see much. There was a line of windows across the front of the building and customers were seated in the booths, but Jericho was nowhere in sight.

"I came here to talk to Alexa," Scottie answered finally. "I thought she'd know about Tasha's funeral arrangements. But then I saw Marcos being brought in by those cops, and I figured it wasn't a good time for her, so I decided I'd have breakfast and wait for him to leave."

Alexa had no idea if any of that was true, but Scottie's eyes watered. She didn't trust those tears any more than she trusted the man.

"I need to say goodbye to Tasha," Scottie sobbed.

"The ME hasn't released Tasha's body," Alexa informed him. "Besides, even if there's a funeral, Tasha wouldn't have wanted you to be there."

"I have to be there." His breath broke. "And I want to see her baby. She's a living part of Tasha and I want to see her face just once."

"You're not getting anywhere near her," Levi said, taking the words right out of Alexa's mouth. Even if Scottie wasn't a killer, he was a stalker, and Tasha had been afraid of him.

"I don't want to hurt the baby," Scottie insisted.

"You're sure about that?" Levi snapped. "Because you seemed obsessed with her when you were at the ranch day before yesterday."

"Because I thought if I had the baby it would help me get Tasha to listen to reason and come back to me."

Yes, he was definitely obsessed. Alexa was thankful Violet was safe and far away from him. Away from Marcos, too. Even though Marcos didn't have anything against Tasha and Violet, Alexa didn't want the baby caught in any more crossfire.

Alexa leaned out to check on Jericho. Still no sign of him, but the diners were hurrying out, so maybe that meant Jericho was having a *chat* with the waitress and busboy. A conversation where they could prove they hadn't tried to poison her.

"Have you found Tasha's killer yet?" Scottie asked, using his shirtsleeve to wipe away his tears.

"No. But you're a suspect," Levi reminded him.

In the blink of an eye, Scottie went from tears to rage. "I didn't kill her! I loved her."

"Maybe you killed her to prove to her just how much you loved her," Alexa suggested, not bothering to hold back any of her sarcasm.

Oh, that didn't help Scottie's temper, but the movement at the front of the diner had them all shifting their attention in that direction. Jericho came out, his hand gripped on the arm of a petite brunette waitress, and he was leading her toward the sheriff's office.

"You recognize her?" Levi asked no one in particular.

"No," Alexa answered. Though she hadn't spent any time at the diner in the past five months. But both Jax and Levi indicated that they didn't know her either.

"She must be new," Mack agreed.

After Jericho came through the door Alexa realized the woman was handcuffed. Mercy. Did that mean she'd admitted to doing this?

"Who are you?" Alexa asked her, and she would have gone closer to the woman, and Scottie, if Levi hadn't held her back.

"I'm Joni Tipton." She didn't look at Alexa. The woman kept her head low and her gaze fixed to the floor.

"She confessed," Jericho explained. "She did put something in the coffee. She claims she doesn't know what it was, but that someone paid her to do it."

"Who paid her?" Alexa demanded.

Still no eye contact.

"I don't know. It was all done through a courier. A guy we called Mouse. Don't know his real name, but the cops at SAPD will probably know him. He called me, said I'd get paid if I did this job. And when I agreed, he brought over the money."

Mack hurried to the phone, no doubt to make a call to SAPD. Maybe it wouldn't take them too long to find and question him.

Jericho put her in the chair next to one of the desks, cupped the woman's chin and glared at her. "Joni, you're in a boatload of trouble. Conspiracy to commit murder will send you to jail for a long time."

The woman didn't seem to have a reaction to that. "I'm already going to jail for a long time. My trial's next week. Drug trafficking. It's my third offense, so it'll be a maximum sentence."

"How the hell did you get a job at the diner with that kind of record?" Levi snapped.

"I lied. Used a fake ID. Said I'd work for free the first couple of days so the boss could see that I'd do good work."

And it'd apparently gotten her hired. "Did you just wait until you had the opportunity to try to kill me?" Alexa asked.

Joni, if that was her real name, nodded. "I was

supposed to get the job done by today, and if you hadn't ordered anything, I was to put it in some coffee, bring it over and say it was on the house."

Judging from the profanity Levi and Jericho used, that might have worked. She knew they ordered takeout from the diner all the time, especially when in the middle of an investigation.

"I couldn't go through with it." Joni whispered it so softly that it took a moment for Alexa to realize what she'd said. "I was about to come over and tell you what I'd done."

"Sure you were," Jericho snarled.

"I was," Joni insisted. "I told Todd I was going to tell."

"Todd?" Jax questioned.

"The busboy," Jericho provided.

"What about the busboy?" Jax asked Jericho. "If she doesn't know who hired her, then maybe he does."

Jericho shook his head. "According to the ID he used to get hired just yesterday, his name is Todd Menger, but he's disappeared. No one saw him leave, and his shift isn't over for another four hours."

"I'm on it," Jax said, taking out his phone. "I need a description."

"Black hair, like I said," Scottie readily provided. "About six feet tall and really skinny and pale. He has a lot of acne on his face. He was wearing a black plastic apron when I saw him in the diner."

"Stay here," Levi told her, and he hurried to the back to check the exit. It was locked, as Alexa had figured it would be, but it was the urgency in Levi's movements that revved up her heartbeat even more.

"Joni Tipton is her real name," Mack called out. "And she's on bail. I'm not coming up with anything on Todd Menger."

"I've told you the truth," Joni insisted.

Jericho got in her face again while Jax and Levi kept watch. "How much did you get paid?"

"Ten thousand." Not much money considering Joni was basically being paid to turn a blind eye to possible murder. "I have a kid. A little boy only two years old, and I needed it for him. My mom said she wouldn't look after him when I'm in jail if I didn't give her money to help take care of him."

Part of Alexa was glad the woman was trying to help her son, but ten grand wouldn't last long, and the grandmother might ditch him after the money ran out. She made a mental note to make sure someone checked on the child.

"Take her to lockup," Jericho instructed Mack. Then, he turned.

Jericho drew his gun.

Both Jax and Levi cursed, and when Alexa

leaned out to see what had caused that reaction, Levi pushed her back into the observation room. But not before she got a good look of the man making a beeline toward the sheriff's office.

He was tall, black hair, and his face was covered with acne. He matched the description to a tee that Scottie had given them of the busboy.

Except for the apron.

He was wearing a white cotton T-shirt and no coat, which made it easy for Alexa to see what he had strapped to his chest.

Sticks of dynamite.

And he held a grenade in each hand.

Chapter Thirteen

"What the hell?" Levi grumbled, and he, too, drew his gun.

Levi hadn't thought this day could get any worse, but he'd obviously been wrong about that. This definitely qualified as *worse*.

"Don't shoot him," Levi warned the others. "If he falls the grenades could go off and set off the other explosives."

Something like that would almost certainly kill Todd Menger, but it could also blow the entire area to smithereens. Levi had no idea how much firepower was in those explosives. The sheriff's office was reinforced with steel inserts in the concrete blocks, but Levi didn't want to test that reinforcement.

"Get down on the floor underneath the table," Levi reminded Alexa.

"Be careful," Alexa said, her voice all breath now. He hated the fear he saw in her eyes. Hated even more that there was a reason for the fear, but he couldn't take the time to reassure her. He had some experience in hostage negotiation and suicides, and while this wasn't a textbook case, he might be able to talk this nut job out of doing something stupid.

"Try to get Marcos and his lawyer out the back exit," Levi told Mack. "Scottie, too."

"Are you crazy? It's too dangerous for us to go out there," Scottie protested. "Those explosives can go off at any minute."

Tough. Levi didn't want to have to watch two of their top suspects while trying to stop this potential disaster.

"Should I go out back and try to come up from behind Todd?" Jax asked.

"No." Levi didn't even have to think about that answer. "If he sees you, he might get spooked and let go of those grenades."

Jax nodded. "I'll call the diner. They can evacuate through the back of their building." He started the call. Jericho made one, too. Probably alerting other nearby businesses so they could clear out, as well.

Good.

He hoped the evacuations would end up being overkill, but Levi wanted people as far away from this as possible. Too bad he couldn't get Alexa out of the building, but this could be another trick to draw her out. She could go right from the frying pan and into a very hot fire.

Levi opened the door just a fraction. Thankfully, the busboy wasn't coming any closer. He was literally standing in the street halfway between the sheriff's office and the diner.

"Todd?" Levi called out. "Is that your real name?"

He nodded. He was hardly more than a kid. Twenty if that, and he was shaking from head to toe. Of course, it was cold, but Levi figured the bulk of Todd's shaking was from nerves.

Not a good sign to have a spooked kid packing explosives.

If his hand started shaking too much, he might drop one of the grenades before Levi got the chance to talk him out of this.

"My last name's not Menger, though," Todd volunteered. "It's Dawson. I want you to know that so somebody can call my family when things are done here. They'll need to know."

Levi didn't have to tell Jericho to do a quick background check on Todd. His brother would. Maybe something would turn up in that check or in something Todd was going to say that would help Levi diffuse this.

"You can't talk me out of doing this," Todd added. "I'm not like Joni, just needing money for her kid. I got to do it. I got no choice."

"You're wrong. You always have a choice. You can put the pins back in those grenades and surrender. That way, you get to live."

Todd frantically shook his head. "No. I'm dying. HIV. It's just a matter of time. I got no life insurance, no money, just a lot of medical bills. This way my girlfriend gets some cash."

Whoever had hired him and Joni must have chosen them because they were both desperate. Well, Levi was desperate, too.

Behind him he could hear Mack ushering out Scottie, Marcos and the lawyer. Scottie was still whining about how dangerous it was to go out there.

"What kind of idiotic plan is this?" Marcos shouted. "Are you trying to get me killed?"

Levi didn't bother to acknowledge Marcos. Instead, he moved a step farther out the door, but Todd jerked back his right hand in a defensive posture, so Levi didn't press it. He stayed put.

"Todd, who's paying you to do this?" Levi asked.

"Don't know. Don't want to know, either." He fired some nervous glances around him. "Mouse brought half the money, and the other half will be delivered to my girlfriend when this is over."

Levi wanted this to have a much better ending than the culprit behind this had planned. To do that, he had to try to gain Todd's trust, be-

cause he couldn't disarm him unless Todd co-
operated. Levi only hoped there weren't other
hired thugs in the area waiting to finish the job
if Todd didn't.

"There are people inside this building," Levi
told him. "In other buildings, too. You don't
want to hurt them."

"Collateral damage. That's what it said in the
note that Mouse gave me. That I was allowed
some collateral damage, and that means it's okay
if other people get hurt or killed. People other
than Alexa Dearborn."

Everything inside Levi went still. Of course
he'd known this probably had something to do
with Alexa, but it felt like a punch to hear it
spelled out by a man loaded with explosives.

"Why are you supposed to hurt Alexa?" Levi
asked.

Another frantic headshake. "I'm not supposed
to hurt her. I'm supposed to make sure she's
dead."

Levi mumbled some profanity. There it was,
all spelled out for him. Alexa, too, probably,
since the observation room door was open and
she'd likely heard every word Todd had just said.

"Think," Levi pressed the man. "Who's Mouse
working for? Who wants you to kill Alexa?"

Todd looked at him. Finally, eye-to-eye contact, but Levi didn't like what he saw there.

Yeah, Todd was shaky all right, but that was determination Levi was seeing. He needed to do something about that—fast.

Behind him, Levi heard someone open the back exit, and Jax immediately pivoted in that direction.

"It's just me," Mack called out. "I put Marcos and the others in a cruiser, and I told them they'd better not get out."

It wasn't ideal, but nothing about this was.

"You said you had a girlfriend, right?" Levi didn't wait for Todd to answer. "Well, Belle, who owns the diner, is someone's girlfriend, and she has a daughter. Only six years old. You want to make that little girl an orphan by killing Belle?"

Todd didn't answer for several long moments. "It doesn't matter. I have to kill Alexa."

"All right," Alexa said.

Levi knew from the sound of her voice that she was no longer in the observation room. And she wasn't. She was coming up the hall directly toward him.

"Have you lost your mind?" Levi snarled at her.

"Possibly, but I'm not going to hide while the rest of you put your lives on the line for me."

Both Jericho and Jax hurried to get in front of her, but she just came up on her toes and looked over their shoulders.

"Can you kill me if you're looking at my face?" she asked Todd. "Can you?"

It wasn't a taunt or a challenge. Just the opposite. There was sympathy in her voice, and Levi didn't expect that sympathy to get through to Todd.

He was wrong.

Todd fixed his stare on Alexa while she stared back at him, and by degrees Levi saw some of Todd's determination fade. He clearly wasn't a trained killer like the hired guns Levi had already encountered and probably hadn't thought he'd have to look his target in the eyes.

Still, Levi didn't want Alexa anywhere near Todd.

"Stay back," Levi warned her.

She didn't listen. Alexa kept her attention nailed to Todd, too. "Does your girlfriend want you to die today?" she asked.

Judging from the groan Todd made, the answer to that was no.

"I'm betting she'd want to spend every possible minute with you," Alexa continued. "The money won't mean anything to her if she doesn't have you."

It was risky because the girlfriend could indeed want the money, but Todd lowered his head until his chin was practically touching his chest, so Alexa had obviously hit pay dirt after all.

Or not.

Todd's head whipped up, and Levi heard a swishing sound. Without warning, Todd dropped face first to the ground.

"Oh, God," Alexa said, and she clearly understood what that fall meant. They could all be dead within seconds.

Cursing, Levi turned, slammed the door shut and dragged Alexa to the floor so he could try to shelter her body with his. He did the only thing he could—brace himself for the blast.

But it didn't happen.

No blast, only silence.

"Todd's been shot," Jax told them. He scrambled for cover beneath one of the desks.

Levi looked up and saw the blood. Hell. Yes, Todd had been shot all right, in the back, and the swishing sound that Levi had heard meant someone had fired the bullet from a gun fitted with a silencer. Todd wasn't moving, but Levi wasn't sure he was dead, either.

"You see the shooter?" Jericho asked, taking out his phone.

Levi didn't see anyone, but it was possible the shot had come from one of the alleys near the diner or even from a roof. No other shots came, but that wasn't Levi's big concern right now.

It was the explosives.

They apparently hadn't gone off because Todd

still had the grenades gripped in his hands. That might not last, though, because all it would take was a slight movement from Todd.

"The county bomb squad unit is on the way," Jericho relayed to them when he finished his call. "But it'll be a while before they get here."

They didn't have a *while*.

"We all need to get out of here now," Levi insisted, and no one argued with him about that.

"I'll get the prisoner," Mack volunteered, and he hurried in the direction of the holding cell where he'd left Joni.

Levi helped Alexa to her feet, and with his brothers right behind him, they ran toward the back exit. When Levi reached the door, however, he didn't just bolt outside. Not with Scottie, Marcos and a gunman out there. With his gun ready, he glanced around.

And Levi saw something he didn't like.

The doors of the cruiser were wide open, and he didn't see anyone inside. Definitely not a good sign, since that was where Scottie and Marcos were supposed to be waiting.

Had they gotten scared and run?

Levi couldn't blame them, but he would have preferred to have eyes on both those snakes. Of course, it was possible they were on the floor of the cruiser, but if so, why had they left the doors open?

Mack came hurrying toward them, and he had a cuffed Joni in tow. The woman looked terrified. Later, Levi would demand that she tell them how much she knew about all this, but that would have to wait.

Jericho motioned toward Jax and Levi. "You should get Alexa in that cruiser. She's clearly the target, and she needs to be far away from here until we can disarm those explosives and catch the person who shot Todd." Then, he looked at Mack. "You go with them and take our prisoner."

Levi did want Alexa away from there, but he didn't want Jericho to stay in a building that could soon be destroyed. "Come with us," Levi insisted.

Jericho shook his head. "I'll wait back here for the bomb squad. Now, go!"

Levi had a quick argument with himself because he didn't want to leave his brother behind, but in the end he knew Jericho was right. Alexa was the target, and that shooter could be coming after her right now.

Or the killer could already be out there in a position to strike.

"Wait here a second," Levi told Alexa, and he stepped out with Jax following right behind him.

Levi went to the left side of the building. Jax to the right. While Mack and Jericho kept watch at the front and the park area behind the sheriff's office.

"Anything?" Jax asked.

"No." There was no one in the parking lot. No one he could spot on the roofs of the other buildings, either. There was also no one on the sidewalk across the street. Jericho's calls to evacuate must have worked.

"It's clear over here, too," Jax added.

That didn't mean a shooter couldn't be hiding, but it was a risk they had to take. Levi only hoped Alexa didn't have to pay for that risk with her life.

Levi hurried back to her, and as expected he saw the fear in her eyes. The worry, as well. "I don't want any of you dying because of me."

Since they were all lawmen, that didn't go over well, and she earned a huff from Jericho. This was their job.

Except it felt like a lot more than just that to Levi.

He surprised her, and himself, when he brushed a kiss on her mouth. Probably also surprised his brothers and Mack, but none of them said anything.

"Don't go out there yet," Levi instructed her as he took the car keys from Mack. "I'll drive the cruiser right up to the back door so you can get in."

"I'll go with you," Jax insisted.

Jax and he hurried out. No one opened fire on them, thank God, but it seemed to take an eternity to go the ten yards or so to the cruiser. It helped that the doors were already open. All Levi had to do was jump in.

When he did that, he immediately saw something else he darn sure hadn't wanted to see.

No Marcos or Scottie. Levi had been right about the cruiser being empty.

But there was blood on the seat.

Chapter Fourteen

Alexa had to remind herself to keep her breathing level. Hard to do with adrenaline still racing through her.

Once again she was hiding out in Dexter's house, and again she was waiting for Levi to finish a lengthy phone conversation with Jericho so she could find out what the heck was going on. With all the other attacks, her imagination was much too good, and she was afraid the worst had happened.

Their escape from the sheriff's office had been frantic and terrifying. Especially once Alexa had seen the blood on the front seat of the cruiser. Whose blood exactly, they didn't know, but that was probably part of what Levi and Jericho were discussing now.

Even with the blood, Levi had driven them out of there fast. First to the ranch so he could get another truck. One he was sure hadn't been tampered with. Then, Jax and Mack had taken Joni to the county jail while Levi and Alexa had gone to Dexter's house. Of course, they'd first had to drive around to make sure they weren't being followed.

The only bright spot in all this was that Violet was okay. Alexa had made sure of that by calling Marshal Walker as soon as Levi and she had arrived at Dexter's. The location of the safe house was being carefully guarded, but she knew from experience that security breaches could happen.

Levi looked up at her from his phone call and their gazes connected, but she couldn't tell from his expression if he was getting good news or bad. There were so many questions and too few answers.

Too many other feelings, as well.

She was getting closer and closer to him, and being under the same roof didn't help. Nor did the fact that she kept ending up in his arms. She wasn't usually so damsel-in-distress-like, but lately she'd felt as if she'd had to fight just to stay alive.

Alexa finally broke down and helped herself to a shot of whiskey from the bottle on Dexter's snack bar. It tasted like battery acid and burned all the way from her throat to her stomach, but it did take off some of the chill. Despite the room being warm, she'd been shivering since they arrived.

Finally Levi finished his call, and he stood and walked to her. But he didn't just go to her. He eased his arm around her waist, inched her to him. Not exactly an embrace of comfort because he put his body right against her. Very unexpected. Like the kiss at the sheriff's office, the one in front of his brothers. It had seemed natural and extraordinary at the same time.

Which more or less described Levi himself.

"How bad is the news?" she came right out and asked.

He lifted his shoulder, rubbed the back of his neck, made a weary sound of fatigue. "Some good, some bad. The bomb squad managed to disarm the explosives. Well, what explosives there were to disarm. The grenades were dummies, and only one of the dynamite sticks was real. It wasn't very powerful, either. If it'd gone off, it would have done some damage mainly to Todd, but it probably wouldn't have hurt anyone else unless they'd been standing right next to him."

She thought about that a moment, but Alexa still couldn't wrap her mind around that. "It doesn't make sense. If the plan was to kill me, then why not load Todd down with real explosives?"

"Maybe because the person behind the attack didn't want to be hurt."

Of course. Both Scottie and Marcos had been in the building. And that led her to another possibility. "Maybe Todd was supposed to draw me out into the open so the gunman could shoot me."

"That did cross my mind," Levi agreed. "But we don't know for sure because Todd's dead."

Alexa had figured as much. He hadn't moved once he'd fallen to the ground.

"There's no sign of the guy who shot Todd," Levi went on. "But an eyewitness from the diner was able to give Jericho a description of an armed man she got a glimpse of when they were evacuating." He paused. "The description matched Lockwood to a tee."

Oh.

Alexa wasn't sure why that rattled her even more. After all, Lockwood was a suspect, but if he'd done this, he'd killed to silence a sick, young man who'd been on the verge of surrendering. And maybe also on the verge of giving them clues as to who'd hired him. It could mean Lockwood had used fake explosives because he, too, hadn't wanted to be blown up during the attack.

"Did Lockwood admit to being in the area?" she asked.

"Yeah. He said he's been keeping an eye on

you, but claims he didn't see the person who shot Todd. Also, the gun he had on him doesn't match the caliber of the bullet used to kill Todd."

That didn't mean Lockwood hadn't disposed of the murder weapon, and it was downright creepy how the man kept following her.

Levi paused again, pushed a strand of hair from her face. "Jericho managed to track down the guy called Mouse that both Joni and Todd mentioned. He's dead. Looks as if he was murdered a couple of hours ago."

Alexa groaned. That couldn't be a coincidence, and it meant the person behind this was tying up loose strings. And that led her to another loose string.

"Whose blood was in the cruiser?" she asked.

"Not sure yet. Jericho's still working that out. We know it's not Scottie's, though. He called to say he got spooked sitting in the cruiser and that he left and ran out through the park. He claims Marcos and his lawyer were okay when he left them, but Marcos isn't returning Jericho's call."

Alexa wouldn't consider it bad news if something had indeed happened to Marcos, but this might be a ploy. Maybe Marcos was even faking his own death with the help of his lawyer. That way he could disappear, start a new life.

And eventually come after her again if he wanted revenge.

"Need another drink?" Levi asked her.

Obviously he knew where her thoughts were heading. A future of always being worried that Marcos might try to kill her. She didn't want him to see that fear in her eyes and started to move away.

Levi held on.

And he delivered another of those extraordinary kisses. His mouth on hers had an immediate effect on her. Like the news, it was both good and bad. She wanted him, but…

"You come with a high price tag attached," she whispered.

"I think yours might be higher," Levi countered.

It was. Being with him would lead to a broken heart for her, but for him this could divide his family along with sending Marcos or whoever was behind this after him. That was plenty of reason for her to step back.

She didn't.

Partly because Levi held on.

"Do you really want to make it through this night alone?" he asked.

The answer to that was easy. "No. But remember that price tag. And no condom," she reminded him.

Levi tipped his head toward the bathroom. "There's a box in the medicine cabinet."

For some reason that made her smile. "A box? How many nights do we need to make it through?"

He didn't smile. She saw only the heat in his eyes. "Probably not nearly enough for this to burn out between us."

She swallowed hard and then lost her breath when he kissed her again. "It'll burn out," she said and tried not to make it sound like a question. It always burned out.

Except the thought came from deep inside her. She'd never had extraordinary. She'd never had Levi.

But apparently that was about to change.

Alexa slipped right into his arms. It was a mistake, of course, but she didn't care. Price tags be damned. She'd deal with the aftermath later and hoped she could survive it. Suddenly, she didn't feel so much like a damsel in distress, but a woman who was about to have the night of her dreams.

Levi kissed her again. Slow and easy as if giving her a chance to run for cover. She didn't run. Alexa felt the heat trickle through her, and for the first time in hours she wasn't cold.

The kisses continued, and soon they weren't so slow and easy. There was an urgency to them, and it caused Alexa to press even harder against him. His grip tightened. So did hers. And it didn't take long for her to want a whole lot more than just kisses and being in his arms.

Levi did something about that. Still kissing her, Levi scooped her up and headed for the guest room. He placed her on the bed as if she were fragile. Like glass. Fitting since Alexa suddenly felt as if she might shatter. He left her for a couple of seconds, and when he returned he had the condoms.

The whole box.

"I should probably tell you up front that I'm not very good at this," Alexa said. "In fact, I don't usually, well, you know. I don't usually."

Good grief.

She couldn't say the word *climax* aloud. She sounded like an idiot instead of a woman who really, really wanted to do this. It was the nerves talking, and they might have kept on talking if Levi hadn't silenced her. With his mouth stretched in a half smile, he dropped down next to her and gave her another of those incredible kisses.

"Let's fix that," he said.

Coming from any other man that might have sounded cocky, but Levi pushed up her top and kissed her in places that made her believe cockiness wasn't involved. First her breasts.

Oh, yes. He knew what he was doing.

Then her stomach.

He lingered awhile there, tasting her and building a very hot fire inside her. Alexa tried to pull him back up to her so she could kiss him, too, but Levi didn't let her. He continued what he was doing.

The kisses going lower.

And lower.

He unzipped her jeans, peeled them off her. Her panties, too. And he took those clever kisses to the center of all that heat.

Alexa quit reaching for him. In fact, she thought maybe she quit breathing. Quit seeing, too. But the rest of her was working just fine. Everything inside her soared. Then pinpointed to where her only focus was on the man delivering some memorable kisses.

She did shatter. But not in that fragile, fall apart kind of way. The pleasure spiked through her until she felt the climax slam through her. Nothing gentle about this. Only the fire and the heat.

Only Levi.

She didn't even have time to regain her breath before Levi made his way back up to her, dropping kisses along the way. Also undressing himself.

Alexa definitely wanted to help with that, and even though she still had a strong buzz from the orgasm, she wanted to see him naked. Now.

And she wanted to touch him, so that was what she did.

"Let's fix that now," she said slipping her hand into his jeans.

He made a sound. A low, manly groan of pleasure that made her feel hot all over again.

Levi pushed her hand away, only so they could get off his jeans. She'd been so right to want to see him like this. Oh, yes. Those Crockett looks gave him his drop-dead hot face, but he had the body to go along with it.

Alexa sampled some of that body. Kissing his chest. Hearing that low sound of pleasure again while he got on the condom. After that it was a blur. A long, slow one when he moved on top of her and entered her.

Again, she lost her breath and didn't care if she lost it a dozen times tonight. Not with the way he was moving inside her. With each stroke she felt the heat return. And build. How could she possibly want him this much when he'd just given her the climax of her life?

And he gave her another one.

She hadn't known she was so close or that it could even happen again so soon. But it happened all right. Levi sent her flying, and with their gazes connected, he said something when he let him go with her.

"We fixed it," he whispered.

True. They'd fixed the fire between them. But as Levi buried his face against her neck, Alexa knew that the fix was only temporary.

So was his embrace. Within seconds, Levi got up and headed to the bathroom. "No, I'm not regretting what just happened," he called out to her. "Give me an hour or two."

Since that was exactly what she was thinking, Alexa nearly laughed. Of course, the slack feeling in her body had something to do with that.

Levi came back into the room. Still naked. And she got a nice view of that hot body that she'd kissed during their scalding foreplay. Alexa considered asking him if he wanted to talk about what'd just happened. Saying aloud all those questions in her head. But Levi silenced those, too, when he got back on the bed and pulled her to him in a body-to-body snuggle.

The questions could wait.

Besides, Alexa wasn't even sure she wanted to hear the answers. Best to hang on to this moment, since she doubted she'd get too many more of them with Levi. Sooner or later he'd come to his senses and regret this, and then there was that whole issue about her being as dangerous as Typhoid Mary.

"Try to get some sleep," Levi said and brushed a kiss on her forehead. "Jericho will let us know if there's a break in the case."

Or if something else went wrong. Which was a strong possibility.

It was that threat of *something else* that made Alexa sure she wouldn't be able to sleep, but apparently Levi's kisses and love making weren't the only things that were extraordinary. The snuggling and his warmth worked a small miracle, and within minutes she felt some of the tension slip from her body.

But not the thoughts.

She wanted more of this. Wanted a real shot at a relationship with Levi. And for that to happen, she needed to end the danger. One quick way to do that was to use herself as bait to draw out the person who was after her. Of course, Levi would never agree to that. However, his brothers might. But if she launched a plan like that, it would pretty much end that real shot at Levi and her having a relationship. The last time she'd gone rogue in an investigation, it'd gotten Paige killed.

Even though it wasn't a loud sound, Alexa still jumped a little when Levi's phone buzzed. "Jericho?" she asked, sitting up.

Levi sat up, too, but shook his head when he looked at the screen. No name just the number. A number she didn't recognize. Levi hit the answer button and put it on speaker.

"You have to help me," the caller immediately

said. It was a woman, but there was a lot of static on the line and her voice was a gravelly whisper. "You have to come and get me before they kill me. I'm at an abandoned hospital. Not sure of the address, but it's maybe twenty or thirty miles from Appaloosa Pass."

Every other word crackled with the static, so it was hard to make sense of what the caller was saying, but Alexa knew the location of that old hospital.

"I can't get into what happened over the phone. Not enough time. But bring Alexa with you so I know I can trust you," the woman added.

"Who is this?" Levi asked.

The woman made a hoarse sob. "Tasha McKenna. I'm alive. But if you don't get here fast, I won't be alive for long."

And the line went dead.

Chapter Fifteen

"I don't like this," Levi said, but he was repeating himself.

"We'll be careful," Alexa assured him. She was repeating herself, too, but no matter how many times she said it, being careful didn't mean they were safe.

Still, he hadn't exactly had a lot of options. If it had indeed been Tasha on the phone, and the woman was telling the truth, he couldn't just let her die. He'd had the option of leaving Alexa behind at the sheriff's office though.

An option she'd declined.

They'd argued, but in the end she had won, only because she'd reminded him of the attack at the sheriff's office earlier that day. The danger, she said, would just follow her, and this might be a way to end it because Tasha might have answers. Answers she hadn't been able to give them because the line had gone dead. Of course, there could be another reason for the no answers part.

Because this was a trap so that someone could try again to kill Alexa.

"You're sure it was Tasha who called?" Mack asked. The deputy was on the passenger's side of the cruiser Levi was driving with Alexa in the middle. He'd chosen that vehicle over his truck because it was bullet resistant, and if it turned out that he had to arrest Tasha, he could restrain her in the backseat.

"I'm sure," Alexa insisted. Something she'd been saying since this latest ordeal had started.

Because Levi had never heard Tasha's voice, he couldn't be certain, but he would trust Alexa on this. What he wouldn't do was trust Tasha. The woman could be luring Alexa into a trap, and that was the reason Levi had brought Mack with him. Jericho and Dexter were following behind them. Four lawmen should be enough, but Levi was wishing he had an army for this.

In addition to the backup, everyone was wearing a Kevlar vest. Everyone was armed to the hilt, including Alexa. As a PI, she'd had firearms training, but Levi hoped she wouldn't have to rely on those particular skills tonight.

"I just don't understand it," Mack continued. "There was a body and it matched the dental records."

"It was obviously faked somehow," Alexa explained. "Tasha will be able to tell us more. If we get to her in time."

Yes, that was a big if. Tasha had sounded terrified, and it wasn't a good sign that the phone had gone dead. Levi had tried to call her back right away, but that call, and the other ones he'd made to her shortly thereafter, had all gone unanswered. The phone number itself hadn't panned out, either, because the call had been made with a pre-paid cell.

"We'll need to do a quiet approach," Levi said, thinking out loud. Just in case Tasha was actually being held at gunpoint, Levi didn't want her captors to panic and shoot her.

He took the final road toward the hospital, and he turned off the headlights when the building came into view. Behind him, Jericho did the same.

The old hospital was on a steep hill. No lights in or around the place since it'd closed years earlier when the new hospital had opened in town. The company that'd bought the place to use as a halfway house had since gone bankrupt, and it'd been at least five years since it had been used.

Well, unless it'd been used by kidnappers.

Levi had to admit, it would be a good place to hold a woman captive. A quarter of a mile from any other building and on a dead-end road. With the bitter cold and late hour, Levi figured there wasn't much chance of anyone being just out for a leisurely drive.

He stopped when he reached the parking lot, and all three of them drew their guns. Levi looked around. No other vehicles in sight. No sign of Tasha, either, but Alexa leaned forward to have a look, as well.

"Tasha won't come out unless she sees me," Alexa reminded him.

Yeah. Tasha had made that clear, but Levi still didn't want Alexa to be an easy target. He waited until Jericho had parked behind him, then Levi opened the door. The interior light came on, and maybe that would be enough for Tasha to get a look inside and see Alexa.

Of course, it might be enough for a killer to see her, too.

Levi didn't get out, but he put one foot on the ground and leaned out while using the door for cover.

Man, it was cold, and the wind snapped and bit at him. But the wind could also do something else he didn't like. It could muffle the sounds of anyone trying to sneak up on them.

The seconds crawled by, turning into minutes, and when Levi was certain he was going to have to go looking for Tasha, a woman leaned out from a broken window at the back of the building.

"Is that Tasha?" Levi asked.

Alexa shook her head, studied her, though it was hard to study a person she could hardly see. The woman was wearing a bulky top and her hair was pulled back.

"Alexa?" the woman called out. "Is Violet all right? Please tell me she's okay. *Please*."

"That's Tasha," Alexa confirmed, and there didn't seem to be any doubts in her voice. "She looks hurt."

She did. Tasha was slumped over, clutching on to the window frame as if she needed it for support.

"Wait here," Levi told Alexa, and he was ready to motion for Jericho and Dexter so they could approach Tasha while Alexa stayed in the cruiser with Mack.

However, Levi didn't even have time to lift his hand before Tasha made a sound. Like a muffled groan of pain, and she ducked back into the building.

Alexa's breath was gusting now and, like Levi, her gaze darted all around. "Do you see what scared her?" Alexa asked.

Levi didn't, but if someone was chasing Tasha, he couldn't just sit there while that someone caught her. And maybe killed her. He got back in the cruiser and drove toward the rear of the building where Tasha had disappeared from sight.

She wasn't near the window. The glass was broken, and there appeared to be some blood on it. Fresh blood because it was still running down what was left of the pane.

Levi drove farther, looking for her. At the back of the building, there were several exits along with plenty of other windows. But only one door was partially open, and that door was just a few yards from the window where he'd seen Tasha. He pulled the cruiser right to it.

He glanced around again to get his bearings. There were a few trees behind the building where a gunman could hide, and the thin moonlight wouldn't help him see if they were out there. But there were also plenty of places for would-be killers to hide inside.

Levi heard a sound, and at first he thought it was Tasha, but it was just the wind causing the old hinges to creak. Definitely not a distraction he needed.

"Is Violet okay?" Tasha called out. She didn't shout. It was more of a loud whisper. That was when he caught a glimpse of her in the hall just off the door. "Please tell me she's not with you because it's not safe here."

"She's fine. Get in the cruiser," Levi ordered her. Yes, it was a risk, because this might be a hoax and Tasha could be armed, but Mack could frisk her as soon as she got inside.

Tasha frantically shook her head, but she did inch closer. This time he got a better look at her face, and she definitely matched the photos he'd seen of her. Except she had cuts and bruises, and she was limping. But not actually limping. There was something on her ankle that stopped her from coming any closer to him.

A chain.

"I can't get loose," Tasha insisted. "The window's as far as I can go. I broke it when I heard your car drive up, but I cut myself on the glass."

Yeah, she had. The woman was wearing a bulky sweater but had shoved up the sleeve on her left arm, and he could see the blood was dripping all the way down to her wrist.

"We have bolt cutters in the trunk," Mack reminded him, and he got out, heading in that direction. "There should be some sort of tourniquet in the first-aid kit to slow the bleeding."

Good, because they'd need both.

"Please help me," Tasha begged.

Judging from the cuts on her face and legs, she had more injuries than just the one on her arm. Or else she'd done a good job of faking those injuries. What she wasn't faking was the shivering. Head to toe. That was real all right. But then it was damn cold, and even though she was wearing that thick sweater and had a blanket on the floor, there was no heat in the building.

"Stay put," Levi warned Alexa. "And, Mack, tell me if you see anyone coming near the place."

It was a risk, but Levi got out. With his gun ready, he stepped inside the old hospital. The smell of mold and dust nearly smothered him. His attention slashed from one side to the other. The place was dark with way too many shadows.

"The men are gone," Tasha said. "For now. But they'll be back any minute. I stole one of their phones to make that call to you, but the battery died before I could explain anything."

Levi had so many questions, but he went with the one that dealt with that phone call. "How'd you get my number?"

"From Alexa. I memorized it."

He glanced back at Alexa to see if that was true, and she nodded.

"Alexa always told me if anything bad happened, that I could trust you," Tasha went on. "I didn't want to call nine-one-one because the kidnappers told me they had a mole in the sheriff's office."

That was an empty threat, but Tasha would have had no way of knowing that. After all, Alexa had been afraid of the same thing when she'd called him to meet her at the Outlaw Bar three nights ago.

Tasha caught on to Levi's arm when he got closer. "My baby." Her fear rippled all through her voice. "Is she safe? Did you tell me the truth? Is she really all right?"

"Violet's fine," Alexa answered. She was still in the cruiser, technically, but the door was wide open, and she was looking directly into the building.

Tasha's breath rushed out. "Thank God." Sobbing, she sank to her knees on the floor.

"Violet's at a safe house," Alexa added. "But we can't take you there—"

"I don't want to go there. Not yet. I can't. I can't bring this danger to her." It sounded like something a frantic mother would say, but Levi still wasn't sure what he was dealing with here.

Jericho and Dexter came in, and Dexter handed Levi the bolt cutters and the first-aid kit that Mack had given him. He also had two flashlights, and he gave one to Levi.

"The men think I'm drugged," Tasha said. "They gave me something right before they left and I pretended to take it, but I spat it out." She motioned toward the two capsules on the floor.

Levi had no idea what was in those pills, but if her captors had indeed managed to drug her, then Tasha likely wouldn't have been able to make that call to him.

"The chain's thick," Dexter said when he examined it. "They've got her tethered to an iron pipe that's fixed to the concrete wall, so it's going to take me a couple of minutes to get her free." And he got busy trying to cut the chain.

Jericho put the tourniquet on Tasha's arm, keeping it loose enough to slow down the bleeding, but not so tight that it could cause permanent damage, and then he stepped back so he could keep watch.

"How is it you're alive?" Levi asked at the same moment that Alexa said, "I saw that man shoot you in the head. I saw you fall, and I saw blood."

"The bullet was some kind of tranquilizer dart. And yes, there was blood because it broke the skin. Then the guy hit me with something. A stun gun, I think." She broke down and sobbed again. "Oh, God. Alexa, if you hadn't gotten Violet out of there, they would have taken her, too."

"But I did get her to safety," Alexa said, obviously trying to calm Tasha down. "Those men that attacked us, did they bring you here?"

Tasha nodded. "They chained me up, drugged me and left me. And then two other men came."

Replacements because the first two had been murdered. "We thought you were dead. There was a body, and it matched your dental records."

Her eyes widened. She started to breathe through her mouth. "The kidnappers must have switched the records."

If so, this had been a well thought out plan, because a switch like that would have had to happen before the kidnapping.

"Then who is the dead woman?" Alexa asked.

Tasha shook her head. "I don't know. But I heard one of the guards talking and he was saying something about a hooker that looked like me, that the hooker wouldn't be missed." Another *Oh, God*. "They killed her, didn't they?"

Probably. But that was something Levi could verify later. For now he needed to get Tasha and Alexa out of here.

"You think Scottie's the one who had you kidnapped?" Alexa pressed.

"Maybe." Tasha paused, shook her head. "But the guard also said something about using me to lure you into a trap."

"Marcos," Alexa said like profanity.

Hell. That wasn't what Levi wanted to hear. Because if that was true, then this could be a trap, as well. Marcos would have known that Alexa would try to save her friend.

"Or Lockwood," Alexa added. She lifted her gaze, looked at Tasha. "I'm so sorry. This is all my fault." It was too dark for him to see her tears, but he could hear them in her voice.

"Maybe not," Levi corrected. "If Scottie is behind this, he could have told the guards to say that so we wouldn't suspect him."

In other words, they still weren't able to rule out any of their suspects.

"Someone's coming," Mack called out, stepping out of the cruiser.

Levi leaned out of the building and handed Alexa the flashlight. He followed Mack's gaze toward the road. A vehicle was indeed driving their way. A light colored van. Both cruisers were out of sight from the main parking lot, but if these were hired guns, they might come around the back.

"We need to move fast," Levi warned Dexter. Not that Dexter wasn't already doing that. He was using the bolt cutters to eat away at the thick chain.

The van continued toward the hospital until Levi could no longer see it. Not good. He didn't know if they'd stopped out front and were already making their way inside. Either way, Levi had a really bad feeling about this.

"Get down on the seat," he told Alexa.

She did. Just as the bolt cutters finally broke through the chain. The second it fell, Levi took hold of Tasha, ready to get her the heck out of there.

"Get down!" Mack shouted before Levi could take a step.

The shot rang out, the bullet slamming right into Mack.

Chapter Sixteen

Alexa could have sworn the gunshot blast roared through every inch of her. And she saw Mack's entire body jolt when the bullet hit him. She prayed that the shot had gone into his Kevlar vest.

But no, it hadn't.

It'd gone into his right leg, and even in the darkness she could see the blood start to spread across his jeans.

Alexa caught on to his arm and pulled him back into the cruiser, but then someone caught on to her.

Levi.

He dragged her across the seat and into the building and did the same for Mack. The moment he had them inside, he shut the door. At least he tried, but the hinges must have been messed up because there was still a gap of several inches.

"I would have had you stay in the cruiser, but I didn't want you to have to drive out of here," Levi told her, his words rushing out. "Because those shooters would have likely gone after you."

Yes, and with Mack injured, she might not have even had him for backup.

Mack hurried inside, but he would have fallen if Jericho hadn't taken hold of him. He sat Mack against the wall and began to rifle through the first-aid kit. Alexa helped with that. There wasn't a second tourniquet, but she unwound some gauze and used that to put pressure on the wound. Maybe it would be enough to stop him from losing too much blood.

"How bad is he hurt?" Dexter asked.

"It's not that bad," Jericho answered, but Alexa wasn't sure if he was lying to keep Mack calm. He called for an ambulance, not that one would be able to get there anytime soon, and the medics wouldn't be able to come into the building until the area was secure.

It wasn't.

Jericho made a second call to the night deputies and Jax and requested backup. Again, it would take time for them to get there, half an hour or more, but at least help was on the way.

There was another shot. This one slammed into the door, nearly making it through that narrow opening. Even though Alexa hadn't seen any gunmen outside, they had probably gotten out of that van.

"Should we try to get everyone back in the cruisers?" Dexter asked.

Levi shook his head. "The shooters are too close."

He was right, and with Mack and Tasha's injuries, they wouldn't be able to move that fast. The rickety door sure didn't help, either, because the third bullet went straight through it.

"We need to move," Levi insisted.

No one argued with him.

Jericho hooked his arm around Mack's waist and hauled him to his feet, and Mack took hold of Tasha. She looked as unsteady as Mack, and both had already lost plenty of blood.

"You remember the layout of this place?" Jericho asked Levi. Years ago this had been the county's only hospital, and all of the Crocketts and just about everybody else in the area had come here at one time or another.

"Yeah." Levi looked at the hall ahead of them and then the one that stretched out on both sides. He tipped his head to the right. "We'll duck into one of the rooms, and when the gunmen come in after us, we can pick them off."

Not a bad plan since they had four shooters, including her, but Alexa had no idea how many gunmen were responsible for those shots tearing into the building. Tasha had said two men had held her captive, but there could be more out there.

They hurried down the hall, and despite the tourniquets, they left a trail of blood behind them. Maybe a trail the gunmen would follow so Levi could put his plan into motion.

Levi tested the doors along the way. All locked. He brought up his foot, no doubt to knock one of them down, but a sound caused them all to freeze.

Another shot.

But this one sounded a lot closer than the others.

That one shot was the only warning they got before the men barreled through the back door. Not two but three of them, all dressed in black and wearing ski masks. They took cover in the recessed area by the hall and started shooting.

Directly at them.

Tasha screamed, but Alexa wasn't sure if the woman had been hit again because Levi pushed Alexa against the wall so she wasn't able to see. In the same motion, he kicked at the door. Across the hall, Dexter did the same to that door. Jericho returned fire, and Alexa would have done the same thing if Levi hadn't muscled her back into place. Protecting her again.

The door that Levi was kicking finally gave

way, and Jericho, Mack, Levi and she all hurried inside. Levi immediately pushed Alexa away from the opening, but she looked behind her, expecting to see Tasha.

She wasn't there.

Neither was Dexter.

Oh, God.

For several horrifying moments, Alexa thought they'd been killed. Then she saw them in the room across the hall. Dexter had obviously gotten through that particular door.

"No windows in here," Jericho relayed to them when he checked out the room. "But there's a door that leads to the next room over. And another door on that side."

Jericho tested the knobs, but both were locked. Good. That meant no one could get through without them hearing them. It also meant they might have an escape route if they got pinned down.

"Do you need the flashlight?" Alexa whispered to Jericho.

"No, and keep it off. If the gunmen see it, they'll know exactly where we are. If they don't already."

Maybe those men hadn't seen which rooms they'd ducked into. But Alexa figured if they didn't know, they'd soon find out.

"Stay down," Levi told her. He took up a position by the door he'd bashed in and glanced out.

Just as a bullet smacked into the wall right next to him.

Alexa caught hold of his jacket and pulled him back, but Levi didn't go far. He was obviously watching to make sure those gunmen didn't get any closer. Or to make sure some didn't come from the other side of the hall. Maybe the person behind this had called for backup, as well.

Two more bullets came.

Then silence.

Alexa wasn't sure which was more unnerving, because the silence could mean the gunmen were on the move. Coming toward them.

She glanced around. It wasn't a big room and had likely once been a doctor's office, since there was still an old desk and a toppled chair. That sparse furniture was the only thing in the room they could use for cover, but maybe it wouldn't be necessary if they managed to shoot any gunman who tried to get in there.

Maybe.

Alexa slipped the flashlight into her pocket and got her gun ready. Waiting. And shivering so much that her teeth were chattering. She was wearing a coat, but the cold seemed to be going straight through it.

She didn't want to think of how cold Tasha

must be. And how terrified. Here Tasha had probably thought she was close to being rescued, but now they were all being targeted by those men in the ski masks. Of course, the upside was that at least Tasha was alive, and that meant Violet wasn't an orphan. Alexa ignored the little tug that caused in her heart.

"It's me," someone called out. "I'm here to help."

Alexa instantly recognized that voice, and it put her heart right in her throat. She wasn't at all sure this was someone who wanted to help.

Because it was Marshal Lockwood.

LEVI WASN'T SURE who groaned louder. Him or Alexa. This was not the kind of help he needed right now.

No way could he trust Lockwood, and it was entirely possible the marshal was one of the gunmen who'd been shooting at them. Especially if Levi went with the theory that the person behind this was using Tasha to draw out Alexa. The timing of Lockwood's arrival was certainly suspicious.

"Lockwood might call off the attack if I offer to surrender," Alexa whispered.

"Not a chance," Levi said.

Jericho added, "No way in hell."

"I wouldn't actually surrender," she argued.

"But if he thought that's what I was going to do, he might let down his guard."

"No, he won't. He's a marshal, and if he's guilty, he'll assume you're trying to trick him."

She shook her head. "But we have to do something fast. Tasha and Mack need to get to the hospital."

"I don't need you to make yourself bait for me," Mack quickly assured her, though each word was indeed laced with pain.

Levi made eye contact with her. Well, as much eye contact as he could manage in the dark room. "I'll find another way," he promised, and hoped like the devil it was a promise he could keep.

"Did you hear me?" Lockwood shouted.

Levi didn't answer, but one of the shooters fired off three rounds. Maybe so they wouldn't think Lockwood was in on this attack. Or maybe because the marshal was genuinely now their target, too.

"Deputy Crockett?" Lockwood tried again.

Levi used the sound of Lockwood's voice to try to pinpoint his location. Definitely not in the same area as the shooters. He was at the opposite end of the hall, maybe trying to close in on them from that direction.

"Don't," Alexa said when Levi made a quick glance out the door. Again, she pulled him back. And again, someone shot at him.

"Did you see Lockwood?" Jericho immediately asked.

"No. The hall's too dark." Especially at that end where there weren't any windows or doors. "I can't see Tasha, either."

Which was a good thing. It meant Dexter had moved her deeper into the room so he could stand guard by the door. That might prevent her from being an easy target if the gunmen rushed them.

Levi's phone buzzed, the sound knifing through the room, and he wasn't exactly surprised when he saw the name on the screen.

Lockwood.

Levi answered it, but he sandwiched the phone between his ear and shoulder so it wouldn't tie up his hands. Now he had to make sure the marshal didn't tie up his attention, as well. Because this call could be a distraction.

"What do you want?" Levi snapped. He didn't sound even a little friendly, but he did keep his voice as low as possible. "And why the hell are you here?"

"I'm trying to help you." Lockwood didn't bother with the friendliness, either, but he did sound riled that Levi had asked him that. "Where are you? I can try to come to you."

That wasn't going to happen. "Where are you?" Levi countered.

Lockwood didn't hesitate. "East side of the building in the hall."

Exactly where Levi had thought he'd be from the sound of his voice. Levi wasn't sure though if the marshal was actually still there since he could only hear him from the other end of the phone line, and Lockwood was whispering.

"How'd you know we were here?" Levi asked, and he listened to try to figure out if Lockwood was moving closer.

Again, no hesitation. "Tracking device on the cruisers and your truck. I put them there during the incident with the gunmen."

Levi had to bite back some profanity. "Why would you do that?"

"Because I wanted to be able to find Alexa if Marcos got to her."

"Or maybe you're the one who wanted to get to her," Levi countered.

Lockwood didn't hold back his profanity at all, and it wasn't exactly a whisper, so Levi was able to determine the man hadn't moved since this conversation had started.

However, Levi couldn't say the same for the gunmen.

It'd been at least a minute since they'd fired a shot, which meant they could be making their move. Levi did something about that. He leaned out just a fraction and fired a shot in their direction. He didn't see the gunmen, but he heard them scurry around, and a few seconds later they sent two bullets right in Levi's direction.

Good.

Levi didn't like getting shot at, but he didn't want to risk being ambushed, either.

"I'm not the one trying to kill Alexa," Lockwood insisted. "And why the heck did you bring her here?"

Levi was asking himself the same thing. Yeah, he'd wanted to save Tasha, but he should have tied up Alexa and left her someplace safe. Too bad someplace safe seemed to be a pipe dream, what with Lockwood monitoring their every move. If Levi had left her at the sheriff's office, Lockwood could have just gone after her there, and Levi wouldn't have been around to protect her.

"Did you shoot the kid with the explosives?" Levi asked Lockwood. "And don't lie. I already know you were in the area."

More profanity from Lockwood. "I was there, but I didn't shoot him. Someone shot me in the arm and I had to get to the ER for some stitches. If you don't believe me, call the hospital."

Oh, he would, but not right now.

"Who shot you?" Levi pressed.

"Don't know. Didn't see him until it was too

late. But whoever it was fired the shot through a silencer."

That would explain why Levi had heard the swishing sound. Well, it'd explain it if Lockwood was telling the truth. It was possible he hadn't been shot at all but was using the injury to make himself look innocent.

"Do you have a plan for getting Alexa out of here?" Lockwood asked.

"Yeah," Levi lied. "The plan starts with getting you out of the building. I don't want you anywhere near Alexa."

Before Lockwood could come back with a quick answer or more profanity, Tasha made a sound. A sharp groan of pain that seemed to echo through the building.

"She hit her arm," Dexter quickly explained.

So, not another injury, but Tasha's groan had been loud enough for Lockwood to hear.

"Is Alexa hurt?" he asked.

"No." And Levi debated how much he should say. He decided to go with the truth to see how Lockwood would react. "It's Tasha who's hurt. She's not dead. Someone's been holding her captive all this time here at the hospital. What do you know about that?"

"Nothing. And that's not right. I saw her body," Lockwood insisted. "Tasha's dead."

The marshal seemed as convinced of that as

Levi had been when Tasha had called him. So, maybe that meant Lockwood hadn't been involved in her abduction, after all. However, that didn't mean he was innocent of coming after Alexa. Lockwood had a very strong motive for silencing her since her testimony at Marcos's trial could end up sending him to jail.

"Hell," Lockwood said. Not a whisper this time. But a shout. "Look out!"

Levi did just that. He glanced out the door to see what the heck had caused Lockwood's warning.

And Levi soon saw trouble.

One of the masked gunmen tossed something into the hall. Metal canisters that immediately rolled toward Levi and the others.

"Shut the door," Levi warned Dexter.

Not a second too soon.

Because the canisters began spewing thick, white smoke right at them.

Chapter Seventeen

Alexa wasn't sure what the gunmen had thrown at them.

Not until she got a glimpse of the smoke.

Not wispy threads of it, either. This was a cloud that spread like lightning over the area.

"Get back," Levi warned her and slammed the door.

Alexa tried to do just that. The smoke was seeping around the sides, bottom and top of the door and filling up the room fast.

Coughing, she scrambled to the back where Jericho was working to get one of the locked doors open. There wasn't a lot of space, what with Mack and the toppled furniture.

Levi coughed, too, but he didn't join her. Instead, he peeled off his jacket and put it at the bottom of the door to cover the gap where most of the smoke was coming in. It would help, some, but it wouldn't be enough. Without any windows in the small room, it wouldn't be long before they were overcome with smoke.

But their attackers probably wouldn't suffer the same fate.

No. They likely had some kind of gas masks or they wouldn't have launched an attack like this in the first place. This was obviously meant to draw them out into the open where they'd all be gunned down.

Once again, this was her fault.

She'd insisted on coming with them, and now because of her, Levi, his brother and two deputies were in danger. And it might all be for nothing. They might not be able to save Tasha, after all.

Alexa stooped down to check on Mack. It was hard to tell, but she thought the bleeding had slowed some. That was something at least. However, that probably wouldn't last when they had to go on the run. Judging from the look in his eyes, Mack knew that.

"Just leave me here," Mack said, his face bunched up from the pain. "You can come back for me when backup arrives."

"You'll go with us," Jericho insisted.

No way would they leave Mack behind. He'd risked his life for Tasha and her, and Alexa would do whatever she could to help him.

"We'll find a way out," she assured him.

Mack nodded. "My aunt's a nurse and used to work here when I was a kid," he said in between the coughs. "I used to play here sometimes, and I'm pretty sure all these offices have connecting doors that lead all the way to east and west halls. Once you're there, you can try to escape through the front of the building."

That was good. If they could make it through them then they'd eventually have a way out. Or at least they could get farther away from the smoke that was slowly smothering them. Of course, if they went east, they'd encounter Lockwood. The last time she'd seen the gunmen, they had been in the west hall.

Either way led to trouble.

But staying put wasn't an option. At least if they made it out of this room, they had a fighting chance.

Jericho cursed when the door wouldn't give way, and he rammed his shoulder against it, not once but twice. Nothing. It held in place. So Alexa joined him, hoping their combined strength would do the trick. Levi went to the other locked door and got to work on it.

"Answer it," Jericho told Alexa when his phone buzzed. He took out his cell and handed it to her.

She saw Dexter's name on the screen and prayed the deputy didn't have bad news about

Tasha and him. With the doors closed between them, she had no idea if they were still even safe.

Alexa pressed the button to answer the call, but since she didn't want the sound of Dexter's voice distracting them from hearing other things—like their attackers perhaps approaching—she didn't put the call on speaker.

"It's me, Alexa," she said. "Are you two all right?"

"For now. How about all of you?"

She was already short of breath from the smoke, and the fear was only making it worse. "We're trying to get out through one of the side doors."

"Tell him to do the same," Jericho insisted. But she didn't have to relay it to Dexter because he clearly heard it.

"There are two doors in this room," Dexter explained. "Only one is unlocked, but it's the one that leads to the east side of the building. I'm heading through it now and will call as soon as I've found a way out."

Alexa knew what that meant. It would get Dexter and Tasha moving away from the smoke. Away from their attackers, too.

But they'd be heading in Lockwood's direction.

"Jax just texted me," Dexter continued. "He's still about fifteen minutes out. The ambulance, too. I told him to be careful with his approach because there might be other shooters out there."

Yes, and she didn't want Jax or the medics driving into the middle of an ambush.

"I'll call when I can," Dexter added, and he hung up.

Alexa relayed that to Jericho, and he cursed. Maybe because he didn't like Dexter's plan or maybe because the blasted door just wouldn't budge. She glanced over at Levi, who wasn't having any better luck.

"Should I help Levi?" she asked.

Jericho shook his head. "I'd rather go through this one and tangle with Lockwood. We can deal with the other dirtbags later."

Yes, of the two evils, she'd prefer Lockwood right now. Well, unless he had backup with him in that east hall.

"Stand back," Jericho said, and he waited only a few seconds before he took aim and fired into the lock.

There was a loud shout. A man. Definitely someone crying out in pain. And for a few terrifying moments, Alexa thought maybe the bullet had ricocheted and hit someone in the room. But the sound hadn't come from one of them.

It'd come from the hall.

Oh, God. Had Dexter been shot?

"You've got to help me!" the man shouted. Not Dexter. But Lockwood. "I've been hit."

No one in the room moved to do anything about that. They were still trying to get the doors open.

Alexa heard a welcome sound. A crack of the wood frame around the door that Levi was battering with his body.

Finally.

Levi had gotten the door opened, but going in that direction would lead them straight to the gunmen. Of course, first they'd have to get through heaven knew how many other doors. And then there were Tasha and Dexter to worry about, since by now they were likely heading toward the east hall. If they got there, they'd be without any backup.

"Toss me the flashlight," Levi said, peering into the dark room.

That revved up her heartbeat even more, something she hadn't thought possible. Had Levi seen something?

Alexa tossed him the flashlight, and as Levi reached to catch it, she saw the movement.

Too late for her to react.

However, Levi reacted all right. He took aim, ready to fire, but he didn't get the chance to do that. Alexa heard the thudding sound.

Levi had fallen to the floor.

THE PAIN EXPLODED through Levi's head, and he got another jolt of it when he fell. His vision blurred. Breath, vanished. But, mercy, he could feel, and it seemed as if every inch of him was hurting.

What the hell had just happened?

Because of the pain, it took him several moments to figure out that there'd been someone in the room, and that someone had bashed him on the head. The person didn't stop there, however. He—and it was a man—knocked the gun from Levi's hand and dragged him to his feet. In the same motion, he jammed a gun to his head.

Levi didn't get a look at the guy's face, but he was big, and his attacker hooked his arm around Levi's neck, squeezing hard so that it was next to impossible for him to regain his breath.

"If you want to stay alive," the man growled, his voice muffled, "you'll do exactly as I say. And don't you dare move a muscle or your girlfriend will get the first bullet. Your brother, the second."

Levi's head was still pounding, making it hard to figure out much of anything, but it sounded as if the guy was wearing a gas mask. Which meant he was one of the hired guns and he'd likely used the smoke bomb as a ploy so he could sneak into the room and come after them.

It'd worked.

Now Levi had to figure out how to undo the damage. And kill this idiot who'd just threatened Alexa and Jericho.

Jericho and Alexa reacted. They both aimed their guns at the goon, but there was no way they could shoot since the guy was using Levi as a human shield. Worse, they were literally out in the open where they could be shot. The only one who was behind cover was Mack, and Levi doubted the deputy was capable of making a shot even if he got the chance.

Dexter might be able to help. *Might.* Of course, Dexter no doubt had his own problems trying to keep Tasha safe. That left backup, and it wouldn't be long before Jax arrived. But it might take his brother a while to find them in the building. Plus, there was the problem of other gunmen. Levi knew there was at least one more, and Jax would have to get past him first.

"Don't come a step closer," the man warned both Jericho and her. "He can live or die. Your choice. If you want him to live, put down your guns now."

The guy did ease up a little on the chokehold, and Levi gulped in several large breaths. Not a second too soon, either. He had been on the verge of losing consciousness.

"Your fight's with me," Levi bargained. "Let the rest of them go."

"My fight's not with you," the guy argued. "And no way am I letting them go. As long as I have them in my sights, you'll cooperate. Now, put down your guns."

Levi saw the debate Jericho was having with himself. No lawman wanted to surrender his weapon, but Levi also knew Jericho carried a backup in a slide holster. That was probably why Jericho finally dropped his primary gun.

"Your turn," the man said to her, and it was a warning. The edge to his voice let them all know he would indeed shoot.

Alexa dropped hers, as well, but it fell only a few inches from her feet. No doubt so she could still get to it.

"Cooperate with what?" Alexa asked him.

Levi didn't want her engaging this guy in conversation. He wanted her to dive behind that desk and try to get out of the path of any bullets this moron might send her way. Levi wanted Jericho to do the same, but his brother stayed put, shoulder to shoulder with Alexa.

"My boss has one demand," the gunman said. "He wants Tasha McKenna. Now, where the hell is she?"

Tasha. Well, that said loads about who was behind this attack. Because only one of their suspects wanted Tasha.

Scottie.

"Scottie?" Levi called out. "Why don't you get in here and speak for yourself?"

It was a risk calling him out like that, but Levi hoped if Scottie was indeed in the building that his arrival would be just enough of a distraction that he could wrestle the gun away from this hired thug.

"Scottie," Alexa repeated. Not a shout. But it was obvious she'd come to the same conclusion as Levi—that Scottie had been the one behind these attacks.

Well, maybe.

It was possible Scottie was only involved in this one, and that meant Marcos and Lockwood could still be responsible for the others.

Levi heard the sound of the footsteps. Not from the office where Jericho, Mack and Alexa were. These footsteps were to his right, and from the corner of his eye, he saw the man step into the doorway. Perhaps Scottie. Levi couldn't tell because the guy was wearing a gas mask.

Levi didn't wait for him to come into the room. He rammed his elbow against the thug's gut, breaking the man's grip just enough so he could pivot, ram him again and get free. It worked.

But not the way Levi had planned.

The goon fired. Not at Levi. But the shot went into the office, directly at Alexa. Levi's heart slammed against his ribs so hard that he nearly lost his breath again. Hell. That bullet couldn't have hit her.

Thankfully, it hadn't.

She lunged to the side in the nick of time, and Jericho went with her, moving in front of her so he could try to protect her.

"You want her dead?" the goon asked, dragging Levi back into a chokehold. He also yanked off his gas mask.

"Of course, he doesn't," the second man answered. "He's crazy about Alexa, and that's why he'll tell us where Tasha is."

Definitely Scottie.

He closed the door behind him and shucked off his gas mask, as well. There was still some smoke, but it was already clearing out. That was the good news. The bad news was that Scottie hadn't cleared out with it.

"Isn't that right, Deputy Crockett?" Scottie continued. "You want to keep Alexa safe."

"Yeah. I want her safe," Levi admitted. "My brother and Mack, too."

Levi didn't mention Tasha and Dexter, but Scottie probably knew they were in the building somewhere. Of course, maybe Dexter had managed to escape with her. If he had, Scottie was not going to be a happy camper. He'd likely take that *unhappiness* out on Alexa, and no way would Levi let that happen.

"You kidnapped Tasha," Alexa said with way too much venom in her voice. It definitely wasn't the tone of someone negotiating for her life.

"*Kidnapped* is such an ugly word. I merely set up the opportunity for Tasha to realize how lucky she is to have me in her life."

Alexa opened her mouth, probably to return verbal fire, but Levi wanted to beat her to it. If someone was going to push Scottie's buttons, Levi would be the one to do it so that Scottie would turn his vicious temper on him rather than Alexa.

"Lucky?" Levi challenged. "You kidnapped Tasha and killed a woman to make us believe Tasha was dead. *Murder*'s such an ugly word, too."

Oh, that got a bad reaction, all right. Scottie stormed toward him, and judging from his tight sneer, he was ready to grab Levi and start punching.

Which was exactly what Levi wanted. Because Levi would punch back—hard.

"Boss, it'll be better if I keep the gun to the deputy's head," the hired thug warned Scottie. "Last thing we need right now is a fistfight."

Scottie stopped in his tracks, but Levi could

still see the struggle for him to rein in that temper. So, Levi decided to push a few more buttons.

"Want to know some other ugly words?" Levi didn't wait for Scottie to respond. "Endangering a baby. You put Tasha's baby in danger when you came after Alexa and me."

The muscles in Scottie's jaw stirred. "I needed the kid. It was the only way I could get Tasha to realize the three of us could be a family."

"It was the only way you could get her to cooperate," Alexa spat out. She looked ready to launch herself at Scottie.

Levi shot her a warning glance, which she probably would ignore, so he got to work again.

"Did it feel good to hurt Tasha?" Levi asked him. "To have your thugs shoot her in the head with a dummy bullet?"

"All necessary," Scottie insisted. "I needed Alexa to believe Tasha was dead or she would have kept looking for her."

"I would have," Alexa snapped.

Scottie shrugged as if he'd made his point. "Now, all I need is Tasha and the kid, and I can make sure all of us have good lives. She's my soul mate, and in time she'll see that."

"Good lives?" Levi challenged. Time for more button pushing. "That's Tasha's blood on the floor in the hall. Your hired thug didn't have a soft touch when it came to handling her."

Scottie made a sound—part surprise, part outrage—and his gaze flew to his thug. "You hurt Tasha?"

The guy frantically shook his head. "No, boss. He's lying. You said don't hurt her, and we didn't."

Scottie came toward him. Not in a rush. Each step seemed slow and calculated. Judging from his enraged expression, Scottie didn't believe the man. Which was exactly what Levi wanted. Scottie was coming closer, and when he was within reach, Levi could grab him and put an end to this.

But that didn't happen.

"Don't shoot," someone called out a split second before the door to Levi's right opened. "It's me, Tasha."

Hell. He hoped the woman wasn't surrendering. Because if she was, Scottie would grab her and order his thugs to kill the rest of them. No way would Scottie leave this many witnesses behind.

Scottie and Levi both turned, and Levi saw Tasha. Clearly shaken. Still bleeding. But she wasn't alone. There was a man behind her, and he had a gun pointed right at her head.

Lockwood.

Chapter Eighteen

Alexa could have sworn her heart skipped several beats. She'd braced herself for another gunman to come crashing through the door, had braced herself also for the fight with Scottie.

But she hadn't expected to see Lockwood holding Tasha hostage.

"Don't let him kill me," Tasha said.

Though Alexa couldn't see Scottie, she heard him, and Tasha's words got him running past his thug and Levi. With his gun lifted, Scottie came running into the room, and he cursed when he saw Lockwood.

"Let her go!" Scottie shouted. "I'll kill everyone here if you don't."

"Go ahead. Kill them," Lockwood said. There wasn't a shred of emotion in his voice, but his body language was sending a different signal.

For one thing, Lockwood was bleeding, and it appeared he'd indeed been shot in his left side.

He seemed steady enough, but he had to be in pain. Tasha, too. Her arm was no longer bleeding, the tourniquet had done its job, but the muscles in her face were tight.

"Where's Dexter?" Jericho asked, and he sounded as dangerous as he suddenly looked. An identical expression to Levi's.

"Your deputy's fine," Lockwood insisted. "He's tied up and probably pissed off that I got the jump on him, but he'll be okay."

"Prove it," Levi insisted.

Lockwood huffed. Or maybe it was a grimace. "Tell them you're all right," he called out.

Several seconds crawled by. "I'm okay," Dexter finally answered.

The relief was instantaneous, cutting through some of the fear, but the fear returned with a vengeance when Scottie pointed his gun at Lockwood.

"Let her go!" Scottie shouted.

Clearly, he was losing it. Not that he had far to go to jump completely off the deep end, but Alexa didn't want him to start a gunfight. Not with Tasha in the middle. Plus, that other thug still had his gun trained on Levi.

"I killed your hired idiot," Lockwood said, looking at Scottie. "That leaves us and idiot number two here."

"Johnny?" the thug called out. Likely the name of his partner who'd helped with this attack.

Nothing. No answer, not even when the thug yelled for him again.

"Told you he was dead," Lockwood explained calmly. "I thought I'd thin the herd before I came in and told you how this is going to work."

"It's going to work by you releasing Tasha," Scottie barked.

"I will. Eventually. You've probably noticed I'm bleeding. That means I'll have some trouble driving off because idiot number one shot me before I could get him. That's where you come in. You come with Tasha and me, and once I'm someplace safe, I'll hand her over to you."

Oh, God. Lockwood was going to use Tasha to bargain for his own freedom.

Maybe.

Lockwood looked at her. Just a glance, but he also lifted his eyebrow. Was he trying to tell her something?

"Do as he says, Scottie," Tasha insisted. "You, me and Lockwood will leave now."

"No." Alexa couldn't say it fast enough, either. "If Lockwood doesn't kill you, then Scottie eventually will."

"I'm not a killer," Lockwood insisted. "But Scottie is. You want to tell the Crocketts how you paid to have Todd and that other woman murdered? Or how you showed up at the sheriff's office to save Alexa from the poison only so you could watch your plan in action?"

Scottie didn't deny any of that, but it explained why those explosives hadn't been lethal.

"Or maybe they're more interested in what you did to Marcos?" Lockwood added.

With his gun still raised, Scottie went closer to Lockwood. "Marcos doesn't matter. Give me Tasha."

Scottie also moved closer to Alexa and Jericho, too. If he came just another foot, she might be able to grab him and get him off balance.

"But Marcos does matter," Lockwood argued. "Go ahead. Tell Levi and Jericho what you did, and then you can leave with Tasha and me."

Scottie stood there, obviously seething. The anger boiling inside him. Maybe it would bring all of this to a head before Alexa could figure out how to stop it.

"Marcos is dead," Scottie said to no one in particular. "His lawyer, too. I thought it best if I didn't have any witnesses to a phone call I got from my stupid employee to tell me that Todd had been shot. I wasn't sure that Marcos actually heard it, but I couldn't take the risk, could I?"

Scottie looked at Jericho then. Smiled. "Good thing you didn't have time to frisk me when I came running into the police station."

She wasn't sure if his story was true, but if it was, Alexa might have cheered because Marcos was no longer a threat. But right now, the danger was greater than ever.

"Let's go with him," Tasha repeated. And she glanced down at Alexa.

Alexa didn't see surrender in her friend's eyes. No. This was something else. The same thing she was seeing in Lockwood's.

Determination to get out of this alive.

This was perhaps a plan to get Scottie out of there so Jericho and Levi could deal with the hired gun. But if that was true, this plan had failure written all over it. Lockwood and Tasha were both hurt, and Scottie might be able to overpower them. If not alone, then he could have another hired gun waiting outside to do that. Tasha could be going from the frying pan right into a deadly fire.

Alexa looked at Mack to make sure he was okay. He was still behind cover. Then she looked at Levi, their gazes connecting. A dozen things passed between them, but she got his silent message. He didn't want her doing anything stupid or dangerous, but that might be the only two options they had left. She gave him a silent message, too. With that gun to his head, she didn't want him moving or trying to fight his way out of this.

Not yet.

But she prayed they'd get an opportunity for that soon.

After all, if Scottie did leave with Tasha and Lockwood, then the hired gun could just start firing. Levi would be his nearest target.

Jericho leaned into Alexa just a little, and she saw him move his hand to the back of his jeans. He was going for his backup weapon, and she needed to do something to make sure Scottie or his man didn't see what was happening and shoot him.

"Tasha, do you really want to do this?" Alexa asked.

Tasha nodded. "It's the only way. If and when you find Violet, take care of her for me."

Scottie jumped right on that. "*If*? There's no if in this. Alexa knows exactly where the baby is because with the help of the Crocketts they hid her from me. That's why Alexa should come with us."

"No," Levi snarled. "Alexa doesn't know where the baby is. None of us do. We wanted it that way so that nothing would be leaked in case someone managed to tap the phones."

Scottie glanced at all of them. Alexa, Jericho, Levi and then Tasha. It was the truth, and Scottie must have sensed that because he cursed and glared at them. "I'll find her. So help me God, I'll find her."

Not that any of them had a say in it. Alexa didn't want this monster anywhere near Violet.

Scottie turned his glare back on Lockwood. "You could just kill me if I go with you," Scottie said.

"I could. But I'm the one holding all the cards here. Or rather the only card that counts for you—Tasha." Lockwood tipped his head toward the hall behind him. "Now let's get moving."

Scottie didn't budge even when Lockwood and Tasha took a step back. "If you walk away from this and leave Tasha with me, I'll tell you the name of the Moonlight Strangler. You'll finally be able to catch him."

Alexa wasn't sure who looked more surprised by that offer. Lockwood, Tasha or her. But Lockwood stopped moving, and his surprise turned to interest.

"How do you know who the killer is?" Lockwood asked.

Scottie smiled. "Connections. Let's just say a friend of a friend put me in touch with him. The Moonlight Strangler and I have had some interesting conversations. I think he might be a fan of mine. I've offered him my assistance if he ever needs it. Like going after Alexa for example."

That sent a new chill through her. "He doesn't want me dead."

"So he said. A pity. But I'm there for him if he ever changes his mind."

It sickened her to think of Scottie in any kind of alliance with the Moonlight Strangler. And maybe he wasn't. There was no proof that the Moonlight Strangler had ever worked with an accomplice.

"Scottie's lying," Tasha said to Lockwood. "Let's just go."

But Lockwood still didn't move. The odds were that Scottie was indeed lying and this was all a ploy to get the marshal to hand over Tasha. However, it had to be tempting for Lockwood to get a shot at collaring a vicious serial killer.

Once, Alexa would have felt the same way.

Not now, though. All she wanted was for them to get out of there alive so that Tasha and Mack could be taken to the hospital.

"Well?" Scottie pressed Lockwood. "Do you want the info or not?"

Either way this wouldn't turn out good for Tasha. Or for them. The only winner in this scenario would be Scottie himself.

With his hand still behind his back, Jericho looked up, snagging Levi's gaze. Levi, in turn, snagged hers. Alexa wasn't sure what was about to happen, but she knew she had to get ready to move.

She didn't have to wait long.

Jericho whipped out his backup, but he didn't aim it at Scottie. He pointed his gun at the man holding Levi. Levi elbowed the guy again and then lunged to the side.

Just as Jericho fired a shot.

The gunman, too, darted to the side, and the bullet slammed into the wall. Levi didn't waste any time tackling him, and the two fell on to the floor just a few inches from her. Unfortunately, the thug managed to keep hold of his weapon, and he landed on hers so that she couldn't get to it.

Yelling like a crazy man, Scottie ran toward Lockwood and Tasha, battering right into them. Tasha screamed out in pain. Probably because her wounded arm had gotten crushed in the assault.

"Here," Mack said, and he tossed Alexa his gun.

She caught it, turned but quickly realized she didn't have a clean shot. Levi and the hired gun were fighting, maneuvering all over the floor and were wedged in the doorway between the two rooms. No way could she risk firing a shot because she might hit Levi.

Jericho didn't have a shot, either, because Scottie had maneuvered Tasha so that she was in between Jericho and him. Worse, Scottie had clamped his hand around that raw cut, and it was clear Tasha was in excruciating pain.

Scottie didn't waste any time creating yet more pain. He bashed Lockwood in the head with his gun. Lockwood cursed and tried to scramble out of the fray, but Scottie would have no part of that. Scottie hit him again.

"Alexa, I was just trying to help you," Lockwood called out. "Now you need to help me."

She wasn't sure she believed him. Nor could she help. However, Jericho did something about that. He tried to latch on to Tasha to pull her out of the way, so Alexa went to help Levi.

Not that there was much she could do.

They were still in a life-and-death fight, and she didn't have a clean shot.

She dropped down on the floor to get herself in a better position, and when Levi punched the man in the face, his head dropped back just enough for her to bash him with the gun.

The shot blasted through the room.

And for several heart-stopping moments, Alexa thought the gun she was holding had gone off and she'd shot Levi. But then she heard the sound behind him and glanced around to see that it wasn't Levi who'd been shot.

It was Lockwood.

Clutching his chest, the marshal fell back.

He slammed into the wall before sinking to the floor.

Scottie didn't waste any time. He latched on to Tasha's hair and dragged her to her feet. He also put the gun to her head.

Levi sprang into action, too. The gunman she'd hit was still dazed, and Levi punched him again. And again. Until the guy quit moving, and Levi ripped the gun from his hand.

"Get down and shoot him if he tries to move," Levi told her. And Levi took aim at Scottie. "You aren't leaving with Tasha."

"Not much you can do to stop it," Scottie said, and he smiled.

Tasha looked at Alexa and shook her head. Now, Alexa saw surrender in the woman's eyes. "Take care of Violet," Tasha mouthed.

Alexa nodded, but she didn't want Tasha to give up the fight. Not yet.

"Take me with you," Alexa told Scottie. "That's the only way you'll get the baby." And it was also a way for Alexa to get Tasha out of this.

Jax was probably somewhere close by, and now that Levi had disarmed the hired gun, it meant both Jericho and he could help stop this disaster in the making.

Scottie stared at her a moment as if considering it. Then, without warning, he lifted his gun.

And fired it.

At her.

Alexa scrambled over the thug, and the bullet slammed into him instead. The man didn't even manage to make a sound. The shot killed him instantly.

If Scottie had any reaction to that, he didn't show it. He glanced over his shoulder and started backing out of the room with Tasha in tow.

Levi clearly didn't have a kill shot for Scottie, but he hurried to the door, only to have to duck back in when Scottie fired at him. The bullet slammed into the doorjamb.

"We can't let him get away," Alexa insisted, but it was something Jericho and Levi already knew.

"You're not getting out this way!" someone shouted. "Scottie, put down your gun now."

Jax.

Judging from the sound of his voice, Jax was in the same part of the hall where they'd first found Tasha.

Scottie cursed and with his eyes widened he volleyed glances among Levi, her and Jax. His eyes widened even more when Jericho doubled around and came out the door where the thug had entered and grabbed Levi.

"This isn't over!" Scottie yelled, and he started shooting.

Levi hooked his arm around Alexa and

dragged her down to the floor, but Scottie just kept shooting. This time at Jax.

Jax didn't return fire, probably because he didn't want to risk hitting Tasha, and Scottie started moving toward the east side of the hall. Alexa already knew from Dexter that there were escape routes there.

Levi moved to the side of the door, no doubt hoping for a better angle for a shot, but before he could even attempt it, Scottie shoved Tasha right at them and took off running.

Tasha landed hard on them, knocking them all back to the floor. Levi quickly maneuvered himself away from them, but before he could take aim, someone else fired.

Oh, mercy.

Had Scottie shot Jax?

Alexa was almost afraid to look. Not that Levi gave her a chance to do that. "Stay down," he warned her again.

And then Alexa heard something she definitely didn't want to hear. Jax's shout.

"Scottie's getting away!"

Chapter Nineteen

Levi wanted to do something to erase the troubled look in Alexa's eyes. In Tasha's eyes, too, but until they found Scottie and put him behind bars, that wasn't going to happen. And everyone in the sheriff's office knew that. All they could do was wait some more, but they weren't doing a good job of it.

Not for the entire three hours they'd been there.

Despite the fact she was sporting thirty stitches in her arm, Tasha was pacing Jericho's office where Levi was waiting with Alexa and her. Every time the phone rang, Tasha held her breath. Of course, she had an even greater reason for wanting Scottie caught.

Violet.

The baby was still at the safe house and would need to stay there until they were sure Scottie was no longer a threat. That meant Tasha wouldn't be able to hold her daughter for the first time in days.

But she would eventually hold her.

Take Violet, too.

Levi wasn't sure why that made his chest ache. Okay, he did know. He'd miss the little girl even though he knew she'd be fine with her mother. From everything he'd seen from Tasha, she loved the baby and desperately wanted her back.

"It'll be okay," Alexa told Tasha. She took her hand, tried to ease Tasha in to one of the chairs, but Tasha only shook her head.

"I can't sit still."

Levi got that. He wasn't sitting, either, though he had finally managed to talk Alexa into doing that. She wasn't relaxing, though. She was waiting on the same pins and needles as the rest of them and worrying that the security measures they'd taken weren't enough.

After leaving the hospital, Levi had called in every available deputy and even two Texas Rangers to help guard Tasha and Alexa.

All but Jax and Mack.

Mack and Lockwood had both been admitted to the hospital where both were in stable condition, and Jax had insisted on going after Scottie. Jax thankfully requested backup from the county sheriff's office. Maybe Jax and the other lawmen would get lucky and track down Scottie.

But there was no need to worry about Marcos. Because he was indeed dead. A jogger had found the bodies of Marcos and his attorney in the park. Gunshot wounds to the head. And since Scottie had already confessed to those two murders, he'd be arrested for those, as well.

Once they found Scottie, that was.

"How many people do you think Scottie killed or had killed?" Levi whispered to his brother.

Jericho blew out a long breath. "Probably a lot more than Marcos, his lawyer and Todd."

Yeah, and maybe there'd be something in his house to prove it. The Rangers were going through the place now.

"You think Lockwood was working for Marcos?" Alexa asked.

"No," Tasha quickly answered. It was yet something else she'd insisted on since they'd gotten out of the hospital. "Scottie told me he'd used a PI to frame him so that Alexa wouldn't trust him."

And it'd worked. "But what about Lockwood holding you at gunpoint and tying up Dexter?"

"Lockwood did both of those things, but the whole time he was doing that he kept saying he wanted to help. He had plenty of opportunities to kill us, and he didn't."

That was true, and if Lockwood had indeed been dirty, taking Tasha hostage wouldn't have solved his situation with Alexa. Or rather the fake situation that Scottie had apparently managed to set up with the PI's false information.

The phone rang, the sound shooting through the room. Jericho snatched it up right away, as he'd been doing with the other calls, but that wasn't exactly a good news expression Levi saw on his brother's face. Jericho stepped into the hall to continue the conversation. Yeah, definitely not good.

Since Alexa looked as if she couldn't handle any more bad news, Levi sank down in the chair next to her and put his arm around her.

"I didn't thank you for saving my life," Alexa said.

Levi shrugged. "I think we're even on that score. I'm pretty sure you saved mine, too."

Her breath broke just a little, and he could see her trying to corral the emotions and spent adrenaline. The tears, too. It'd be a while before she won that particular battle.

Because he felt they both could use it, he brushed a kiss on her cheek, then her mouth. Her breathing became uneven again, but this time Levi didn't think it was from the adrenaline. Despite their dark cloud situation, it gave him a rush to see the heat in her eyes.

Soon, he wanted to do something about that. Something more than the obvious of just hauling her off to bed. But Levi was still mulling over exactly what that something should be.

"I don't want to risk losing you again," he told Alexa.

Though he did say it a lot louder than he'd intended. Tasha's gaze quickly darted away, and she moved her pacing further away from them. Not that she could go far. The room wasn't that large.

Alexa didn't dodge his gaze. "Does this have to do with what happened between us? The sex, I mean," she added in a whisper.

"Yes." But Levi immediately shook his head. "Maybe not, though."

Maybe it had to do with the feeling that he should be discussing this with her in private. This was clearly making Tasha uncomfortable, and the woman had had to deal with enough without having to listen to Levi say…

Well, he still wasn't sure what to say, but it would probably involve something for Alexa's ears only. That meant it was time for a change in subject, and there was only one subject that would help with the tension in the room.

"You think Violet's keeping the protection detail up tonight?" Levi asked. "Your daughter doesn't sleep that well," he said to Tasha.

That got the reaction he wanted. Alexa smiled. Tasha, too, though hers was very short-lived. "I can't ever thank you both enough for saving her and taking care of her." Something she'd been repeating a lot for the past couple hours.

"We were glad to do it," Alexa insisted.

Levi was surprised that it was true for him, as well. He only hoped he got a chance to see the baby one more time.

Tasha paced some more. And Levi figured he could do something to give them all a little peace of mind.

He texted Marshal Walker at the safe house and asked him to use the secure computer to set up a temporary feed between them and the sheriff's office. Once that was done, Levi turned Jericho's laptop in Tasha's direction and the baby's image popped onto the screen.

Violet was awake all right.

Marshal Walker had the baby in his arms and was rocking her.

Despite the horrors Tasha just endured, the pain and worry vanished from her face. Though tears did spring to her eyes, Levi was sure they were the happy kind. While smiling and crying, Tasha leaned closer and touched her fingers to the screen, caressing her baby's face.

Levi saw the love in Tasha's eyes. Not that he'd doubted it. When they'd first arrived at that abandoned hospital where she was bleeding and being held captive, the first thing Tasha had done was ask about Violet.

Jericho stepped back in the room, his attention not on them, but on someone in the squad room. A moment later, Dexter came in and handed Jericho what appeared to be a fax.

"They found Scottie," Jericho said when he turned back toward them.

That got their attention, and Levi issued a quick apology to the marshal, telling him he'd text him when it was okay to resume the video feed with Violet. Even though Violet was way too young to know what was going on, Levi didn't want her to hear this. Or to pick up on her mother's fears if Tasha broke down.

"Scottie's dead," Jericho added.

The relief was instantaneous. Alexa collapsed against Levi, and Tasha finally sat down and buried her face in her hands.

"Thank God," Tasha prayed, and she just kept repeating it.

Levi was saying some prayers of thanks, too, but that wasn't exactly a thankful look Jericho was giving him. "What's wrong?" Levi asked his brother.

Just like that the relief vanished, and both Alexa and Tasha snapped their attention in Jericho's direction.

"Scottie was already dead when Jax found

him," Jericho continued. "He'd been strangled and had a crescent-shaped cut on his cheek."

Levi knew that MO. It belonged to the Moonlight Strangler. Alexa knew it, too, because the color drained from her face.

"Yeah." Jericho looked at Alexa. "The Moonlight Strangler left a message for you on Scottie's body. Are you up to seeing it?"

"Of course." Though she didn't sound exactly sure of that.

Nor did Jericho jump to hand her the fax. "The message isn't written on paper."

Hell.

Levi took the fax, had a look for himself, and he saw the words carved on Scottie's chest and stomach.

"A favor for you, Alexa," the message said.

Alexa read it, as well, and Levi braced himself for the fallout. But it didn't come. She looked up at Jericho. "Did anyone see the Moonlight Strangler at the scene?"

"No," Jericho quickly answered. "Scottie had been dead at least an hour before Jax found him."

"Good. Scottie deserved to die," she said. "At least this way, Scottie wouldn't have had a shot at hurting Jax or the other lawmen after him."

Levi was thankful for that. They'd all been through way too much for Scottie to have hurt anyone else. Still, Levi hadn't expected to have the Moonlight Strangler as an ally in any situation, including this one.

"So, it's over?" Tasha asked.

Jericho nodded. "Jax was able to make a positive ID of the body. Scottie's really dead." He paused a heartbeat. "Would you like to see your daughter now? I can drive you out to the safe house?"

Tasha sprang to her feet before Jericho even finished his offer. "Yes, please. Take me to her." She turned as if to hurry out of the room, but then she stopped and looked at Alexa and Levi. "Would you like to go, too?"

Alexa glanced at him, obviously trying to figure out what to do, but then she shook her head. "This should be your moment with Violet, but after you've picked her up, maybe you can bring her back here so we can see her?"

"Of course." Tasha moved again but then stopped. "I guess I'll need a hotel room. I don't have a place nearby to take her."

"You can stay at the ranch," Levi offered. "There's a guesthouse, and you can use it as long as you need. The protection detail can go ahead and take you there, and Alexa and I can meet you."

"Thank you." That brought on more happy tears, and Tasha hugged him, then Alexa before Tasha took hold of Jericho and got them moving.

"You think you can talk Tasha into moving to Appaloosa Pass?" Levi asked.

Despite everything that'd happened, Alexa smiled again. "Probably. She doesn't really have any other place to go. Why? Do you want to keep Violet nearby?"

"Absolutely."

His quick answer widened her smile, and Alexa slipped into his arms, causing him to smile. "So do I." And she kissed him. Or maybe he kissed her. They moved toward each other at the same time and sort of met in the middle.

As all their kisses were, this was darn good, but before it continued, Levi had to make sure of something. "Are you okay, really?"

"Well, that kiss helped. *You* help," Alexa added, giving his arm a gentle squeeze.

Levi stared at her, waiting for the truth. "That doesn't answer my question."

She hesitated. "I suppose I should feel bad that so many people are dead."

"No, you shouldn't, since two of those people probably would have come after you again if they'd been given the chance."

Alexa stayed quiet a moment, nodded. "At least this way you and your family are safe. Tasha and Violet, too."

That was a huge deal as far as Levi was concerned, and he wouldn't lose a minute's sleep over the death of a piece of scum like Scottie.

"Let's get out of here and get some rest," Levi offered. "It'll be a couple hours before Tasha makes it to the safe house and then back to the ranch."

Levi called out to Dexter to let him know they were leaving, but then Alexa stopped in her tracks. "Wait, I don't have any place to go, either."

"Yeah, you do." He kissed her to give her a hint of where that place might be. His house. His bed.

"You're sure?" she asked.

He was. But Levi was also positive of something else. "I don't want this to be temporary."

"What? The sex?" she asked in a whisper.

It probably wasn't a very manly reaction, but Levi huffed. "Yes, the sex is important, but I don't want any of this to be temporary." He made a circling motion around them.

She stared at him for what seemed to be an eternity. "Good. Because I'm in love with you, and it's not temporary."

And with the bombshell she would have headed out the door if Levi hadn't hooked his arm around her waist and stopped her. "Wait a minute. What did you say?"

"I'm in love with you," she repeated as if it were the easiest thing in the world to say. It wasn't.

"Does this have something to do with us nearly dying tonight?" he asked.

"No." She dropped a kiss on his lips, caught on to his hand and got him moving toward the back door. "I figured it out before that. When we were in bed."

Oh.

"Well, hell," he grumbled.

Alexa stopped, faced him and flinched a little. "Look, if you're not happy about my being in love with you—"

Levi cut off the rest of that with a kiss. A really hot, long one. "I'm happy about it, all right. I'm not happy that it took me longer than you to figure it out."

Her smile came. Slow and easy. "But you did figure it out. That takes us out of the temporary zone for sure."

It did. But Levi wanted a heck of a lot more than that. He only hoped he could convince Alexa of it as he led her out of the building and toward his truck.

"We could take things slowly, just date for a while," he tossed out there. "And my family would have to work through each event—also slowly. You coming to Sunday dinner with all of us. You sleeping with me, of course."

Alexa stared at him. "Will I be doing all that?"

Levi nodded. "And with you moving in with me, too. I want you to move in with me. Tonight."

"Is that your idea of taking things *slowly*?" Alexa asked.

"Well, we don't have to make the sex slow. We can manage that after you've had some rest. The moving-in part, too."

Alexa kissed him, pulled him to her and, feeling her body against his, Levi thought maybe that rest was seriously overrated.

"Then what will we take slowly?" she pressed.

"Getting married. I figure that's the next step to us getting our little version of Violet. Which, of course, means lots and lots of sleeping with me."

"Best plan ever," she said, making him a very happy man indeed. "So, just how slowly should this go?"

He checked his watch. "When we wake up in the morning, I'll ask you to marry me. Is that slow enough?"

Alexa laughed. Kissed him. "Perfect timing. Because in the morning, I'll say yes."

Levi figured that gave him about eight hours, more or less, and he scooped up Alexa in his arms so they could get started.

* * * * *

LARGER-PRINT BOOKS!

HARLEQUIN

Presents®

PASSION GUARANTEED SEDUCTION

GET 2 FREE LARGER-PRINT
NOVELS PLUS 2 FREE GIFTS!

YES! Please send me 2 FREE LARGER-PRINT Harlequin Presents® novels and my 2 FREE gifts (gifts are worth about $10). After receiving them, if I don't wish to receive any more books, I can return the shipping statement marked "cancel." If I don't cancel, I will receive 6 brand-new novels every month and be billed just $5.30 per book in the U.S. or $5.74 per book in Canada. That's a saving of at least 12% off the cover price! It's quite a bargain! Shipping and handling is just 50¢ per book in the U.S. and 75¢ per book in Canada.* I understand that accepting the 2 free books and gifts places me under no obligation to buy anything. I can always return a shipment and cancel at any time. Even if I never buy another book, the two free books and gifts are mine to keep forever.

176/376 HDN GHVY

Name	(PLEASE PRINT)
Address	Apt. #
City	State/Prov.	Zip/Postal Code

Signature (if under 18, a parent or guardian must sign)

Mail to the **Reader Service:**
IN U.S.A.: P.O. Box 1867, Buffalo, NY 14240-1867
IN CANADA: P.O. Box 609, Fort Erie, Ontario L2A 5X3

**Are you a subscriber to Harlequin Presents® books
and want to receive the larger-print edition?
Call 1-800-873-8635 today or visit us at www.ReaderService.com.**

* Terms and prices subject to change without notice. Prices do not include applicable taxes. Sales tax applicable in N.Y. Canadian residents will be charged applicable taxes. Offer not valid in Quebec. This offer is limited to one order per household. Not valid for current subscribers to Harlequin Presents Larger-Print books. All orders subject to credit approval. Credit or debit balances in a customer's account(s) may be offset by any other outstanding balance owed by or to the customer. Please allow 4 to 6 weeks for delivery. Offer available while quantities last.

Your Privacy—The Reader Service is committed to protecting your privacy. Our Privacy Policy is available online at www.ReaderService.com or upon request from the Reader Service.

We make a portion of our mailing list available to reputable third parties that offer products we believe may interest you. If you prefer that we not exchange your name with third parties, or if you wish to clarify or modify your communication preferences, please visit us at www.ReaderService.com/consumerschoice or write to us at Reader Service Preference Service, P.O. Box 9062, Buffalo, NY 14240-9062. Include your complete name and address.

HPLP15

LARGER-PRINT BOOKS!
GET 2 FREE LARGER-PRINT NOVELS PLUS
2 FREE GIFTS!

◈ HARLEQUIN®

Romance

From the Heart, For the Heart

YES! Please send me 2 FREE LARGER-PRINT Harlequin® Romance novels and my 2 FREE gifts (gifts are worth about $10). After receiving them, if I don't wish to receive any more books, I can return the shipping statement marked "cancel." If I don't cancel, I will receive 4 brand-new novels every month and be billed just $5.09 per book in the U.S. or $5.49 per book in Canada. That's a savings of at least 15% off the cover price! It's quite a bargain! Shipping and handling is just 50¢ per book in the U.S. and 75¢ per book in Canada.* I understand that accepting the 2 free books and gifts places me under no obligation to buy anything. I can always return a shipment and cancel at any time. Even if I never buy another book, the two free books and gifts are mine to keep forever.

119/319 HDN GHWC

Name	(PLEASE PRINT)	

Address		Apt. #

City	State/Prov.	Zip/Postal Code

Signature (if under 18, a parent or guardian must sign)

Mail to the **Reader Service:**
IN U.S.A.: P.O. Box 1867, Buffalo, NY 14240-1867
IN CANADA: P.O. Box 609, Fort Erie, Ontario L2A 5X3

Want to try two free books from another line?
Call 1-800-873-8635 or visit www.ReaderService.com.

* Terms and prices subject to change without notice. Prices do not include applicable taxes. Sales tax applicable in N.Y. Canadian residents will be charged applicable taxes. Offer not valid in Quebec. This offer is limited to one order per household. Not valid for current subscribers to Harlequin Romance Larger-Print books. All orders subject to credit approval. Credit or debit balances in a customer's account(s) may be offset by any other outstanding balance owed by or to the customer. Please allow 4 to 6 weeks for delivery. Offer available while quantities last.

Your Privacy—The Reader Service is committed to protecting your privacy. Our Privacy Policy is available online at www.ReaderService.com or upon request from the Reader Service.

We make a portion of our mailing list available to reputable third parties that offer products we believe may interest you. If you prefer that we not exchange your name with third parties, or if you wish to clarify or modify your communication preferences, please visit us at www.ReaderService.com/consumerchoice or write to us at Reader Service Preference Service, P.O. Box 9062, Buffalo, NY 14240-9062. Include your complete name and address.

HRLP15

LARGER-PRINT BOOKS!
GET 2 FREE LARGER-PRINT NOVELS PLUS
2 FREE GIFTS!

HHARLEQUIN®

super romance®

More Story...More Romance

YES! Please send me **The Montana Mavericks Collection** in Larger Print. This collection begins with 3 FREE books and 2 FREE gifts (gifts valued at approx. $20.00 retail) in the first shipment, along with the other first 4 books from the collection! If I do not cancel, I will receive 8 monthly shipments until I have the entire 51-book Montana Mavericks collection. I will receive 2 or 3 FREE books in each shipment and I will pay just $4.99 US/ $5.89 CDN for each of the other four books in each shipment, plus $2.99 for shipping and handling per shipment.*If I decide to keep the entire collection, I'll have paid for only 32 books, because 19 books are FREE! I understand that accepting the 3 free books and gifts places me under no obligation to buy anything. I can always return a shipment and cancel at any time. My free books and gifts are mine to keep no matter what I decide.

263 HCN 2404   463 HCN 2404

Name	(PLEASE PRINT)	
Address		Apt. #
City	State/Prov.	Zip/Postal Code

Signature (if under 18, a parent or guardian must sign)

Mail to the **Reader Service:**

IN U.S.A.: P.O. Box 1867, Buffalo, NY 14240-1867
IN CANADA: P.O. Box 609, Fort Erie, Ontario L2A 5X3

MMLPBPA15